DIRTY MINDS

A J.J. Graves Mystery

LILIANA HART

ALSO BY LILIANA HART

Whiskey on the Rocks

Whiskey Tango Foxtrot

Whiskey and Gunpowder

Whiskey Lullaby

The Scarlet Chronicles

Bouncing Betty

Hand Grenade Helen

Front Line Francis

The Harley and Davidson Mystery Series

The Farmer's Slaughter

A Tisket a Casket

I Saw Mommy Killing Santa Claus

Get Your Murder Running

Deceased and Desist

Malice in Wonderland

Tequila Mockingbird

Gone With the Sin

Grime and Punishment

Blazing Rattles

A Salt and Battery

Curl Up and Dye

First Comes Death Then Comes Marriage

Box Set 1

Box Set 2

Box Set 3

The Gravediggers

The Darkest Corner

Gone to Dust

Say No More

Published by 7th Press
Dallas, TX 75115

To Scott—Wow! So much has happened in the last year. We have a house full of love, we've raised five amazing kids, and the dogs mostly listen when we tell them to do something. I'm so excited to move into this next season of life with you.

ACKNOWLEDGMENTS

Getting a book to publication takes an amazing team of people. I'm fortunate to have had these people in my corner for years.

To my editors—Imogen Howson and Ava Hodge for always making me better.

To my cover designer—Dar Albert for always blowing me away with your talent.

To my children—You're all so special. You have gifts and abilities beyond measure, and I'm excited to see what God has in store for each of you.

To Scott—thank you for answering a ridiculous amount of law enforcement questions and acting out weird scenarios with me. Any mistakes are mine alone.

Dear Readers,

I started writing the J.J. Graves series back in 2009, and I never could have imagined we'd come so far. We've been together for thirteen books—through despair and joy, love and heartbreak, laughter and tears—and you're still here with me.

I don't have words for what your devotion to this series means to me (which isn't easy to admit for a writer). And I can't tell you how special it is to get emails letting me know some of you have read these books through cancer treatments, or during the hard times when you needed an escape, teachers on summer vacations, or moms sneaking chapters during nap times.

Books are meant to touch us in the deepest parts of our souls, and we connect with characters because we see something special in them—something we see in ourselves or a trait we long to possess.

So thank you from the bottom of my heart. I truly feel like this is a family we all get to be part of. Enjoy Dirty Minds!

All my love,
Liliana Hart

The bitterest tears shed over graves are for words left unsaid and deeds left undone.

—Harriet Beecher Stowe

Murder is unique in that it abolishes the party it injures, so that society has to take the place of the victim and on his behalf demand atonement or grant forgiveness; it is the one crime in which society has a direct interest.

—W.H. Auden

CHAPTER ONE

THE PURPLE PIG HAD ONLY BEEN OPEN A FEW months, but the locals seemed to love it. Maybe it was the vivaciousness of the atmosphere, or maybe it was because of the neon purple pig on the front of the building. But whatever the case, the place was hopping on a Friday night.

King George County was growing away from the silent, sleepy place I'd grown up in. Its proximity to both DC and Richmond made it not too terrible of a commute for those who wanted to raise families away from high crime and politics, and when tobacco farming had become unpopular over the last couple of decades, a majority of the landowners had sold their property to big developers.

Back in 1945 there had been over two thousand farmers producing tobacco. Less than a hundred years later there were fewer than two hundred. Someone famous once said that progress was impossible without change, and those who couldn't change their minds couldn't change anything. There were a lot of residents who'd tell you they were just fine with their minds the way they were, so progress in King George had been about as slow as the *Titanic* trying to avoid an iceberg.

But the Purple Pig was a sign of progress, and the prime location across from the courthouse assured that young attorneys and clerks and others who worked downtown would make their way over after work for happy hour to consume cheap drinks and have a good meal before heading home. The atmosphere and hospitality was what had them staying to pay full price after happy hour was over.

My name is J.J. Graves, and I wouldn't consider myself trendy or hip, and I wasn't sure where I fit on the progress side of things. I tended to stay in my own lane for the most part. I liked going to work and then going home. I preferred NASCAR-style grocery shopping where I got in and out without having to talk to too many people. And I liked drive-thru windows and self-service gas stations. There was a reason I worked with the dead.

But marriage had changed me—some—and I had to admit I enjoyed the new conveniences that had been popping up around town. It was nice to have grocery stores and gas stations that stayed open after the sun went down, and it was nice to have restaurants that didn't have fifty years of grease caked on the floor, though Martha's Diner was still thriving for those who preferred the good old days.

Which was how I'd come to be at the Purple Pig on a Friday night, in the midst of a rambunctious happy hour, with a group of people I called friends. I closed my eyes and breathed in the atmosphere—the smell of beer and the yeasty bread they served on all the tables, the clink of glasses, the raucous laughter. There were some things worth savoring.

Lily sat to my right. She was one of those people you couldn't say no to, and it had been her suggestion to let off some steam after work. I knew cops pretty well, and it took a lot for them to agree to being shoved in a crowded room where reaching for their weapon would be interesting if the situation called for it. But Lily had a way of getting people to agree to things they didn't necessarily want to do. It was a good thing she used her powers for good. Otherwise, she would've been a menace.

Lily had just started her graduate work, and after a short hiatus, she'd come back to work for me as assistant coroner. She'd somehow managed to turn the boring black suit she'd worn to work that day into a date night dress that had Detective Cole drooling into her very bountiful bosom. Lily was one of those people who turned heads no matter where she went, and if it wasn't for Cole sitting protectively with his arm across her shoulder, several of the men eyeing her from the bar would've been crowding our space.

We were all still getting used to the idea of Cole and Lily as a couple. Their age difference was a factor, not to mention cops weren't typically the best bet for relationships, but to all of our surprise, they'd connected on a deeper level. And after Lily had been kidnapped by a serial killer and had been rescued by the skin of her teeth, it had been plain for anyone to see that Cole was more than just infatuated. Now we were just waiting to see if he recognized it, and whether or not it would scare him into running the opposite direction.

Jack sat on my other side with his back to the corner. His chair was tilted back on two legs as he carried on a lively conversation with Martinez about baseball. Martinez had also maneuvered his chair so his back was against the wall, and even though Jack and Martinez were talking to each other their eyes constantly scanned the room looking for potential threats.

Jack's arm was draped over the back of my chair and his other hand balanced a bottle on his knee. It wasn't often Jack was relaxed, and I was glad to see he'd let the worries of the last couple of days slide away—at least for a moment.

Tom and Emmy Lu sat across from Lily and Cole. Tom and Emmy Lu weren't cops or in the business of death, so it was odd they'd made their way into our merry band of misfits, but the donut king and my receptionist had been grafted in as if they'd always been there. I wasn't sure what they were all talking about, but Lily and Emmy Lu were crying with tears of laughter.

And at the very end of the table was my assistant Sheldon Durkus, his eyes wide behind his Coke-bottle glasses and his cheeks pink with embarrassment over whatever Lily and Emmy Lu were laughing about.

I exhaled—content—and let it all soak in around me. It had been a hard week, and things would get harder in days to come. But it was good to forget, at least for a little while.

I looked at the almost empty plate of nachos

in front of me and debated on whether or not to order dessert. I would regret it, no doubt, but I couldn't start a weekend without dessert. A weekend where we didn't have any plans. A weekend Jack and I would get to spend alone since Doug had decided to go visit his mother. A weekend where there were no funerals scheduled, no bodies in my lab, and no social events planned.

As if Jack were reading my mind, he squeezed my shoulder lightly and kept up his commentary about a strike and money and things that seemed ridiculous considering they were talking about a game, but I leaned into him and felt the smile spread across my face.

I didn't recognize the person I'd become over the last couple of years, but I liked her. I liked that we were surrounded by friends and the bonds that had formed between us were deep and long lasting. I liked the woman who hadn't given up, who'd fought the demons inside of her until she was whole and free. And I liked the woman who'd learned how to love—who was still learning—and who'd finally found the joy that had always seemed just out of reach.

The large plate-glass windows at the front of the restaurant were like living frames for the outside world. I watched a steady stream of people bustling along, leaving work or meeting friends for drinks, shopping or passing people they knew and stopping to chat. The neon sign cast them all in a purple hue. Many of them decided to come inside, and all stopped to stare at the ridiculously gaudy crystal chandelier that hung over the bar. But it somehow added to the charm of the place.

There was a boisterous six-top in the front corner that caught my eye. More so, it was the woman in the red dress that caught my eye. I didn't recognize her, but gone were the days where you knew every person you came across in town. She was young—very young—with gorgeous white-blond hair she wore up in a messy bun, and her dress was thin and strappy and not at all appropriate for the cold temperatures outside. There were several empty drink glasses in front of all of them, and they'd been knocking them back steady since they'd come in.

She didn't look old enough to drink, but the others at the table looked like professionals who'd spent a long day at the office, and the fit older man with silver hair who had his shirt sleeves rolled up to show off sinewy arms had become increasingly cozy with her as the drinks flowed and the time passed.

"You asleep, Doc?" Martinez asked, signaling to the waitress to bring him another drink.

It hadn't gone past any of our notice that Martinez was drinking more since his partner's death a few months ago. He'd also started working more nights and overtime whenever he could get it. He was fighting his own demons and we all knew he was on a fast path to destruction if he kept going the way he was.

"Nah, just thinking about dessert," I said. "And wondering how soon that couple at the front table is going to leave so they can do it."

"Twenty bucks they'll be in the bathroom in five minutes," Martinez said. "I've been watching them too. He's old enough to be her grandpa."

"Looks like he's in good shape though," Lily said. "I'll take that bet. He looks like a professional. Probably an attorney. He won't do it in the bathroom. They'll do it in the car." Then she winked. "It's classier that way."

"And how are we supposed to find out who wins?" Cole asked. "I wouldn't be surprised if they did it at the table. She took her panties off half an hour ago. Someone should go card her. She doesn't look old enough to drink. Or arrest them for public indecency."

"Not it," Martinez said quickly. "I'm off the

clock this weekend. I've got big plans that don't involve any paperwork."

"The manager has it under control," Jack said, nodding toward the sharply dressed man in all black. "He's been watching them. He won't let it go too much further. And he carded her before she ordered."

"You never miss a trick," I said, shaking my head.

"What about you, boss?" Cole asked. "You getting in on this bet?"

"The only bet I'm taking part in is whether or not Jaye gets dessert," Jack said. "Though I'll double down that she'll regret it. She's not as young as she used to be."

I narrowed my eyes and glared at him. "I'm not old. And I *am* getting dessert. They have apple pie. It's healthy."

His lips twitched. "I hope you don't give people this kind of medical advice."

"My patients are all dead," I said. "They can eat what they want."

Martinez snorted out a laugh. "I've noticed your appetite is more vigorous than usual, Doc. Maybe you've got an announcement you want to make."

The table got quiet and everyone turned to stare at me. Jack got very still beside me and I knew his face would be impassive. I was clearly on my own for this one.

"No," I said firmly. "I have no announcements. I'm a stress eater." My tone was defensive and everyone started smiling, as if they were in on a secret that I wasn't privy to yet. Though I was pretty sure I'd be the first to know about the announcement they were waiting for.

"It's Emmy Lu's fault," I said. "She keeps bringing donuts to work and we've been neck deep in bodies lately. Anyone would have cravings after that."

I'd apparently used the wrong word choice because their smiles got bigger. I sighed with defeat. To be fair, Jack and I had been talking about starting a family. And we'd been practicing a lot for when we wanted to put our plan in motion. But practice was as far as we'd gotten.

I looked at Jack and he smiled and shrugged his shoulders, making it seem like everyone had found out our secret.

"Seriously?" I asked him. "You're not going to help me out here."

"I'm just a simple man," he said, grinning. "Enjoying the simple things in life."

I elbowed him in the ribs just as the waitress came over. "I'll have an apple pie," I told her.

"And a beer to go with it." Then I pointed at Jack's bottle. "Whatever he's having."

That seemed to deflate the conversation, and everyone else gave their dessert orders and refilled their drinks.

"Just for that, I'm not sharing my pie with you," I said to Jack.

"Sure you will," he said. "You know you never finish it." He leaned in and kissed the corner of my mouth. "You're cute when you're flustered. Maybe we should take our dessert to go."

"Mmm," I said, snuggling closer. "I like the way you think."

Cole interrupted the moment and said, "You lose, Martinez." He nodded toward the couple at the front table. "They're putting on their coats. I've got to agree with Lily on this. I bet they do it in the car."

"I'm changing my vote," Lily said, shaking her head. "Now that I've got a better look at him, he seems like he's compensating. I bet he drives a Porsche or something. A guy his age can't do it in a car that size. They'll go back to her place. She probably lives in one of the new apartments around the square. I bet he's married. What a jerk."

Martinez let out a low whistle. "Lady, if you got *any* of that right I'll give you a hundred bucks. Someone who has that kind of skill should be profiling for the FBI. You sure as hell don't need to be wasting talent like that in the pathology department."

There were several boos and hisses at the mention of the FBI. We weren't fans of the FBI at the moment, despite the fact that Jack's best friend was—or had been—one of the higher-ups in the organization. Things were complicated and we were still sorting out the details.

I nudged Jack and said, "Hurry and ask for the check. All I can think about now is eating our dessert at home."

Jack laughed and kissed me just above my ear. "You're so easy."

"I'm trying to be," I said cheekily.

That's when all hell broke loose.

The first plate-glass window exploded inward, spraying shards of glass in every direction. There were screams and tables were upended as people threw themselves on the floor and glass rained down like glowing purple diamonds. It was then I heard the rapid-fire gunshots and every window across the front shattered.

Jack shoved my chair to the side and I hit the floor before I even realized what he'd done. I instinctively covered my head with my hands, but changed positions when I felt him move. I watched in terror as he and Cole and Martinez pushed our tables over to use as a kind of shield and then they ran toward danger instead of hiding like the rest of us.

It had all happened in a matter of seconds. And then there was an eerie silence.

"Everyone stay down," Jack yelled. And then the screams started.

Jack and Martinez and Cole were already in motion, Jack peeling off toward the alley entrance and Cole and Martinez going out the front. I'd noticed Officer Jackson was in another part of the restaurant with his girlfriend when we'd first come in, and he was only a few steps behind Cole.

I pushed up on my hands and knees and got to my feet. Glass was everywhere, even in my hair, and I took quick stock of my body to make sure I was in one piece.

"Lily," I yelled over the chaos. "You okay?"

She was on the floor where Cole had shoved her and she had a dazed look in her eyes, but she nodded her head in the affirmative and tried to get up.

Then I heard the kind of scream I was all too familiar with. Death tore something in the souls of those who witnessed the violence of it first-hand, and I shuddered as the wails of those who'd cheated death crawled across my skin.

I'd spent too many years in the ER for instincts not to kick in.

"Lily, call 911 and tell them we need an ambulance. Sheldon, run to the Suburban and grab my bag. Tom and Emmy Lu, block the exits until Jack can get back so no one slips out. They'll need to talk to everyone."

I tossed Sheldon my keys and they hit him in the chest and bounced to the floor since his glasses were skewed, but I knew he'd get himself together and get moving. I'd found giving people something to do in a crisis kept them functional instead of paralyzed with fear. I climbed over the table and stepped over people until I got to the source of the sound.

"Let me through," I yelled. "I'm a doctor."

I knelt down beside a woman who was huddled next to the victim, her arms over her head protectively and her body shaking with tremors. It was the woman in the red dress. I hadn't recognized her with her coat on.

"Ma'am," I said, taking her by the shoulders. "Let me see. I'm a doctor. Let me help."

She went limp and I was able to push her out of the way enough that I could see what I was dealing with. It was the silver-haired man, also dressed in his coat and scarf, and his keys were still clutched in his hand.

Even I could see there was nothing a doctor could do for this man. There was a bullet hole in the center of his forehead.

CHAPTER TWO

"Paramedics are on the way," Lily said, coming up behind me. She looked down at the victim. "Yikes. I'm going to change my shoes. My feet are already killing me. And I think I've got some coveralls in the car. I'll be right back."

I grunted in agreement. We were going to be here for a while, and the heels Lily was wearing weren't crime scene friendly. For some reason, television had decided that every female cop and coroner must work every scene in a two-thousand-dollar leather jacket and spiked heels. Which only told me that no one in TV had ever spent any time on an actual crime scene or enjoyed the luxuries a first responder salary provided. The work was long and tedious and there was a lot of standing involved. Then there was the added bonus of crime scenes like this one where glass littered the ground and it was easy to slip and slide.

"I need everyone to move back," I said. "Is anyone else hurt over here? What about you?" I asked a thin pale man who'd uprighted a chair and was sitting with his elbows resting on his knees and his head down. He had smeared blood on his pressed khakis and along the cuffs of his dress shirt.

He held out his palms faceup to me and said, "It's just glass. I landed on my hands."

"You'll want to get that cleaned out when the EMTs get here," I said. "Make sure you go see them."

Miraculously, it seemed no one else on this side of the restaurant had been injured other than minor abrasions and lacerations. I'd worked a number of drive-by shootings when I'd worked the ER at Augusta General and I'd been expecting a bloodbath.

"You," I said, pointing to one of the victim's companions. He was a sturdy man with thick blond hair and tortoise-rimmed glasses, but more importantly, he seemed to have most of his wits about him. "I need to go see if anyone else needs help. What's your friend's name?"

He glanced down at the body at my feet and

swallowed. And then he said, "David. David Sowers."

"I need you to make sure everyone stays away from David until I get back. No one touches him. Can you do that?"

He nodded and I had no choice but to take him at his word. I could feel the internal *tick, tick, tick* of the seconds that passed. Counting seconds during an emergency was like breathing to me. Only minutes had passed since the first shot had been fired and every single second was critical. There was nothing I could do for David Sowers, but maybe someone else had a fighting chance.

"Over here," I heard someone yell.

I looked across the room and saw the manager waving in my direction. He stood at the opposite corner of the bar and was pushing people back who were starting to move around. I saw out of the corner of my eye a couple try to slip out the front door only to be met by Tom Daly, and I knew he'd be able to get them corralled back inside until Jack returned.

Almost all of the liquor bottles behind the bar had been broken, and the smell of alcohol permeated every surface. The chandelier hung haphazardly and crystals littered the ground. My shoes crunched over broken glass as I made my way to the manager, and I was glad I'd gone with my sensible black boots that morning.

"You're the manager?" I asked the man in black. He skimmed just under six feet and was built like a boxer. He had a square head, a five o'clock shadow, thick black hair, and eyes so dark I couldn't see his pupils.

"The owner," he corrected. "Alex Denaro. I got up as soon as the dust settled to see who needed help. This lady seems to be the worst of it."

I moved the heavy barstool out of the way and squatted down beside her. There was a lot of broken glass around the bar, mostly from glass-ware and bottles. I hadn't noticed her while we'd been eating, but the bar had been at least three people deep the last time I checked.

Her body was curled protectively around the corner of the bar and all I could see was crimson. There was a good amount of blood spatter arced across the front of the bar, and I shot into action.

I looked around to see if Sheldon had made it back with my medical bag, but it was hard to see anything from my current line of sight and Denaro was blocking most of my view while standing guard.

"If you see a small guy with glasses come in with a black bag tell him I need him fast," I said to Denaro. "And if you see the medics pull up tell them I need them faster. I need towels and something I can use for a tourniquet in the meantime."

I didn't wait to see if Denaro followed my instructions. He was cool under pressure, and I knew he'd get things taken care of.

The woman's eyes wheeled up at me and I could see she was going into shock from blood loss. I placed two fingers at the base of her neck and felt the rapid pulse.

Denaro handed me a stack of dish towels from behind the bar and a scarf he must've taken from one of the other patrons.

"This'll do," I said. "Thanks."

I got to work. There was three inches of glass protruding from her arm, and she had several deep-level lacerations that had most likely penetrated to the bone. The blood spatter on the front of the bar was from the brachial artery being severed.

I didn't even have a pair of gloves with me. I moved quickly, removing the glass and simultaneously applying pressure with the dish towels.

The woman whimpered with pain and I said, "I know that hurts, but I've got to press hard."

"Can I help?" Denaro asked.

He'd moved back from behind the bar and was kneeling across from me.

"Apply pressure," I said, elevating her arm and demonstrating how I wanted him to do it. "Harder than you think it needs to be. The artery needs to press against the bone. She's already lost too much blood."

Once he took over applying pressure, I tied the scarf around her arm tightly.

"Pretty handy having you here tonight," Denaro said casually, but I could see the sweat dotted on his forehead.

"The Lord works in mysterious ways," I said, making him chuckle. "This wouldn't normally be my Friday night hangout."

I didn't think anything of it. Cops laughed over crime scenes all the time. Not in a disrespectful way, but because it was a natural way for the brain to deal with trauma. They called it gallows humor for a reason.

I kept my fingers on her pulse, and my brow furrowed with concern. She needed to be in surgery. There wasn't much else I could do for her.

"I didn't think I'd ever seen you here before," he said. "But I recognized you and the sheriff. Next time let me know you're coming. Your whole night will be on the house. I got a soft spot for first responders."

I heard the sirens and breathed out a sigh of relief. "Just hang on," I whispered to the woman. "Help is on the way."

I looked up at Denaro and said, "You've handled this like you've done it before. There aren't many people who can get shot at, have their business destroyed, and still keep their wits about them long enough to keep people calm and help where it's needed."

He smiled, showing square white teeth and bringing some charm to his stoic nature.

"Yeah, well, let's just say my family has a few Italian mob ties. This isn't the first time I've seen something like this."

"You think this was mob related?" I asked.

"Nah, I don't think so," Denaro said. "I've been out a long time. My family and I live a quiet life here."

I nodded, but tucked the information away so I could share it with Jack. "Anyone else you can think of that could do something like this?"

"Hard to say," he said, shrugging. "I haven't always been an upstanding businessman, but I keep my nose clean now and haven't had any issues for a dozen years or so. We bought a place in Bloody Mary last year." He rolled his eyes. "My wife watches too many of those home and garden shows. Thought we'd do better buying some old place in the country we could fix up. But I'm a city boy at heart. This place was my attempt to feel a little more at home."

"It's a great place," I said and then I looked toward the door and saw Sheldon. The paramedics were right behind him.

"Madi!" I called out to the woman in the navy BDUs and matching zip-up shirt. She wore a ball cap to hold back her dark ponytail. I'd worked several scenes with her and her partner, Jeff. "We've got a critical!"

I moved out of the way so they could get the gurney close.

"What have you got?" Madi asked.

"Severed brachial artery," I reported. "She's in shock. Pulse is rapid and BP falling. She's lost a lot of blood."

"Got it, Doc," Madi said. "We'll take care of her. Lucky for her you were here. Triage is being set up outside for anyone with minor medical needs."

I nodded and Denaro and I moved out of the way so they could get to work. It was then Jack came back inside. I could tell by the look on his face they hadn't caught the ones responsible. I could also tell he was pissed.

Cole, Martinez, and Jackson came in next,

and they spread out through the room, trying to get things organized so they could take statements from those who weren't injured and send anyone else to the triage center.

Jack headed straight for me and I moved to meet him halfway.

"You okay?" he asked.

"Not a scratch," I said. "You didn't find him?"

He shook his head. "I've got units out searching, but we found an empty SUV down the block. He had alternate transportation and is gone for now. Witnesses on the sidewalk said it was only one shooter. Caucasian male. Black glasses and a black ski cap. Black Escalade with dark tinted windows. He used a submachine gun in short bursts. I was listening for full auto, but he was in control. We'd have had a lot more fatalities otherwise."

"That's a lot of damage for one guy," I said. "And an expensive choice of vehicle. The owner tells me he's got Italian mob ties, but he said he's been out of the game a long time. Sounded like more of a family legacy. He and the wife moved to Bloody Mary last year."

Jack arched a brow and then he looked over my shoulder as Denaro encroached on our space.

"Alex Denaro," he said, reaching out to shake Jack's hand. "This is my place. Once I told the doc a little of my past I figured you'd have to look into it. It's a natural connection."

"But you don't think it was mob related?" Jack asked.

Denaro shook his head. "Not their style," he said. "My family tends to be a little more dramatic. Believe me, I'd know if it was them. There'd be a lot more blood and a lot more bodies. And they've accepted that I'm no longer in the game. Which means I'm no longer part of the family. I stopped existing to them a long time ago. I had to build everything I have from the ground up. I didn't have a cent to my name and had no place to live. Didn't even go to my grandmother's funeral. I've built my own empire."

"Can you give us some names?" Jack asked. "Just so we can eliminate and aren't wasting our time?"

"Sure," Denaro said. "As long as you don't go stirring the hornet's nest. You don't need those kind of problems. Know what I mean?"

"I hear you," Jack said.

"I'll get you a list."

Jack nodded. "You know anyone who owns a black Cadillac Escalade?"

Denaro's brows furrowed in thought. "Not off the top of my head," he said. "But we don't know a whole lot of people here. We're not exactly country club material, and I've been putting all my time into this place. But it doesn't ring a bell as far as any of the regulars."

"Thanks," Jack said. "I'll let you know if I've got any other questions. One of the other guys will grab an official statement from you."

"I'm not going anywhere," Alex said. "Whatever you need. Seems like a good time to pass out free drinks to these people since insurance is footing the bill for this fiasco." He nodded and went to the back room.

"Everyone in here will be wasted before you can get their statements," I said.

Jack's lips twitched. "I'll tell the guys to work fast. How many fatalities do we have?"

"One," I said, nodding to the other side of the restaurant where Lily had taken control of things. "Victim's name is David Sowers."

"We'll run him," Jack said.

"Then we can see how accurate Lily was in her predictions," I said smirking. "Our vic is the old guy with the lady in the red dress."

Jack's lips twitched. "You don't have to look so excited about it."

"I'm not saying it's good he's dead," I clarified. "I'm just saying it's fortuitous that the victim will allow the bet to be settled. There's nothing we can do for him now but discover the truth."

"Convenient," Jack said.

"What about victims on the street?" I asked. "There were people on the sidewalk and on the courthouse lawn."

Jack shook his head. "No fatalities. Minor injuries, and one guy with a flesh wound from a ricocheting bullet. It's pretty incredible. It was a risky operation. King George County isn't exactly known for its gang activity, which is usually who's responsible for crimes like this."

"What's incredible to me is that there was a drive-by that did this kind of damage, and we only have one victim. The guy must be a terrible shot."

Jack grunted and looked down at my hands. I followed his gaze and realized I was covered in blood.

"From the victim?" he asked.

"A woman who fell on a drinking glass and severed her brachial artery. She's being transported for surgery. Her chances are much better than they would've been if she hadn't gotten help in time."

"Good thing you were here," Jack said.

I blew out a breath. "People keep telling me that. I guess it's a good thing you didn't listen to me when I suggested we leave town for the weekend."

"You only suggested that after Lily invited everyone to this place," he said. "Don't think I didn't realize you were trying to come up with some last-minute out-of-town trip we'd forgotten to tell everyone about."

I huffed out a breath. "Well, don't you wish you'd gone along with it now? We could be halfway to Miami right now and the beach."

"You may have a point," Jack said. "Next time I'll go along with your lie."

"It doesn't sound as nice when you say it."

He just smiled.

"Come on," I said. "Let's go take a look at our victim."

Lily had cleared that side of the room and one of the crime scene techs that was now swarming the place had blocked off the area with crime scene tape. She'd found her coveralls and sneakers and was gloved up and looking at the wound in the center of our victim's forehead. Sheldon stood against the wall, clutching my bag to his chest.

She didn't bother looking up at us as we joined her. "Entry wound is nice and neat," she said. "Exit wound is a nightmare. The back of his head is missing."

"Huh," Jack said, narrowing his eyes.

"What?" I asked.

He took a step back and then started looking among the rubble and glass on the floor. "I need forensics over here," he called out.

I took my bag from Sheldon and dug inside for gloves. I passed a pair to Jack and then put on my own, and then I handed him an evidence bag and some tweezers. He grunted his thanks, but I could already tell he was in his own world.

Jack squatted down and carefully picked up a copper bullet fragment out of the glass, and then he dropped it into the evidence bag.

The forensics team was suited up and ducked under the crime scene tape. "People are getting crazier all the time," one of the guys said. "Heard you were here to tell the tale, sheriff."

"Word travels fast, Carter," Jack said. "We got lucky this time. I find I'm rather aggravated about the whole thing. I found this fragment here on the floor." He held up the bag. "Do me a favor and extract one of the bullets from the back wall."

"You got it," Carter said.

"What's going on?" I asked.

"This is a fragment of a hollow point .308," Jack said. "This is the bullet that killed our victim."

"How can you be sure?" Lily asked. "We're going to find a lot of bullets in here."

Sheldon cleared his throat and took a step forward like he was giving a report. "Did you know the Red Army had over two thousand female snipers in World War Two?"

"This is a sniper shot?" I asked, surprised.

"Here you go, sheriff," Carter said, handing Jack another evidence bag. "Nine-millimeter."

"That's what I thought," Jack said. "Sounded like a MAC-10."

"So we have two shooters?" I asked. "A guy with a sniper rifle and a guy driving a black SUV not hitting a single person with a semiautomatic weapon."

"A distraction," Jack said, nodding. "Which tells us that our victim here was the real target."

CHAPTER THREE

"Talk about planning," I said. "Looks like the killer really wanted to make a statement."

"He's showing off," Jack said. "Picked a crowded place, and it would've been a challenging shot, especially with how close this guy was cozied up to the red dress. So the killer's got training. Maybe military. Though he would've been trained to go for center mass instead of the head shot. But again, he's showing off. He even knew what kind of rounds to use so the bullet didn't kill anyone else on the pass-through."

"And he just hires a guy for the drive-by to cause chaos so he can get the shot off?" I asked.

"Something like that," Jack agreed. "Martinez!"

Martinez handed off the interview he was in

the middle of to another cop and jogged toward us.

"What's up?" Martinez said.

"Hollow point .308," Jack said, showing him the bag.

"Sniper," Martinez said, raising his brows and letting out a whistle. "Ballsy."

"Take a team and canvas the area," Jack said. "See if you can pinpoint where the shot originated from."

"On it," Martinez said, calling out names of the officers he wanted to go with him.

I squatted down next to David Sowers and inspected the entry and exit wounds. I knew I'd find fragments of the bullet inside his brain when I did the autopsy. That's what Jack had meant about the killer knowing the kind of rounds to use so no one else was killed. The hollow point bullet went in small and then came apart once it made impact, basically scrambling the brain like eggs until it exited, making a big mess on the way out as it ran out of steam.

I checked his pockets and came away with a wallet, which I handed over to Jack, a wedding ring, cell phone, a monogrammed money clip holding at least a thousand dollars, and a prescription bottle.

"What's that?" Lily asked.

"Performance enhancement," I said. "Guess he decided he didn't need it tonight."

"Why do you say that?" Lily asked.

"Because he'd still be ready for the party, even in death," I told her. "I haven't found any car keys."

"He probably valeted it," Jack said. "Anything else?"

"Fountain pen in the shirt pocket," I said. Then I reached inside his jacket pocket and pulled out a small vial half full of white powder.

"Well, well," I said, holding it up so Jack could see. "What do you think?"

"I think he had big plans for the night, and we need to talk to his lady friend," he said, and then he took the victim's wallet out of the bag. "ID says his name is David Michael Sowers. Age sixty-one. Has a King George address. I'll have one of the guys run his license and pull up his plates so we can find his car."

"We know just from watching him he'll be over the legal limit of alcohol," I said. "But it'll be interesting to see what else he's got in his system. His clothes are expensive. Designer label suit and shoes."

"I'll add to our wager and put money down that he's an attorney," Lily said. "Probably a regular here. Easy enough for his staff or co-workers to walk over from the courthouse, and it's far enough away from King George Proper that his wife probably won't check up on him. I was right about that, by the way. Him being married, I mean."

"Martinez is going to be sad," I said. "He hates losing."

"Then he should never bet against me." Lily grinned. "I know things. I come from a long line of medicine women. My grandmother could clear up syphilis or make your hair fall out, depending on how well she liked you. And how much you paid her," Lily said, winking.

I laughed and then checked the tissue around the nose and inside the nostrils. "Evident inflammation of the mucous membranes and some broken capillaries. I'll check for needle marks, but he seems like a high-end junkie. They typically don't like to inject. Let's get him bagged up and back to the lab."

"You got it," Lily said. "Sheldon and I can take care of it. You two go do what you do. If you see Cole tell him I'll meet him back at his place and we can trade massages."

"Not it," I said, touching my finger to the end of my nose and looking at Jack.

"Real mature," he said, but I could tell he wanted to laugh. Then he looked at Lily. "How about I don't tell him that and you can surprise him. Men love surprises."

Jack put his hand on my back and led me away before she could respond.

"What if Cole hates surprises?" I asked.

"Then they don't know each other as well as they thought they did," he said. "This is a growing opportunity. Let's talk to Denaro. I don't see the woman in the red dress."

"Maybe she's in the back," I said. "What about that woman talking to Cole? She was at the victim's table. Maybe she knows something."

Jack grunted and headed toward Denaro. He was on the phone and just hanging up as we approached.

"Insurance guy is on the way," he said. "I guess we're already on the news. He was the one who called me."

"Sounds like good service," Jack said.

"Not in my experience, but maybe this place is different," he said.

"You know anything about our victim? Ever seen him before?"

Alex nodded and said, "Sure, every Friday like clockwork. The rich junkie. I caught him doing lines in the bathroom once and told him to keep that stuff out of my place or he's not welcome back. He got all puffed up about it and started using a bunch of legal terms, but I pulled Karen out from behind the bar and told him this was my place and my rules and that my next call would be to the cops."

"Who's Karen?" I asked.

Alex smiled and reached under the bar for a Louisville slugger that looked like it had made impact a time or two with a ball or a skull. "Meet Karen. She was a gift from my grandfather when I turned thirteen. You can take the boy out of the mob, but not the mob out of the boy. Know what I mean?"

"Sort of," Jack said. "What about the girl? He ever come in with her before?"

"Just the last two weeks," Alex said. "I'd never seen her before then. I thought she might be his daughter at first, but then...well, obviously she wasn't. I carded her but license said she's legal, so we served her."

"You think it was fake?"

"I don't think so," he said. "I'm pretty good at spotting them. Hell," he said, grinning, "I used to make them. I've made it a point to card her each time she's ordered though. It's our policy, even if we recognize the customer. She's shown the same license each time."

"You remember her name?" I asked.

"Bethany Wildes," Alex said. "But the dead guy called her Bethie."

"He bring a lot of young girls in like that?" Jack asked.

"He always brought somebody," Alex said. "Not that young, but always younger than him. And usually with his same crew of people. They always sat at that front corner table. I've seen a couple of them walk over from the courthouse a time or two."

"But not the victim?" Jack asked. "He never walked across?"

Alex snorted. "Nah, that guy is all about the show. Liked to drive his fancy Porsche and flip the keys to one of the valet guys. And then he leaves here loaded and high every week and squeals out like a maniac. It's a miracle he hasn't killed anyone."

Another score for Lily, I thought to myself.

"Have you seen the girl around here?" Jack asked. "We'd like to ask her some questions."

"Yeah, I bet," Alex said, raising his brows. "I haven't seen her around. No one is in the back but some of the kitchen crew cleaning up."

"Thanks," Jack said. "You've been a big help."

Cole was still talking to the victim's friend, so we headed in that direction next, but we ran into Officer Jackson on the way.

"Hey, sheriff," Jackson said. "We're wrapping up statements. Maybe have a dozen or so left."

I didn't know Jackson well. I wasn't even sure of his first name. He was one of the many cops I saw around the station from time to time, and one that kind of flew under the radar since Jack had never mentioned him working any particular cases. He was a tall, dark-skinned man with the kind of biceps and shoulders that filled out a shirt nicely.

"I'm looking for Bethany Wildes," Jack said. "She was with the victim. Red dress. You seen her?"

"I know who you're talking about," Jackson said, nodding. "Hard not to. My girlfriend and I saw her come in. She took off that coat and I swear half the restaurant dropped their silverware when they saw that red dress. Or what there was of it. Anyway, I haven't seen her. She's not on my list. Martinez might have got to her first since she was with the vic."

"Thanks, I'll check with him," Jack said. "You come here often?"

Jackson shrugged and said, "We've been a few times. My and Charlotte's schedules don't always line up too good. She's a NICU nurse. Never noticed the girl or the victim before. But this seems to be a decent place. Owner has things under control and doesn't let anything slip by."

Jack nodded and Jackson went off to take his next statement.

"Paperwork on all this is going to suck," I said.

"You can say that again," Jack said. "Looks like Cole is finishing up."

"Sheriff," Cole said when we headed over. "This is Jasmine Taylor. She's acquainted with the deceased."

For whatever reason, Cole was using his country boy charm and his drawl was heavier than usual.

Jasmine was a pretty woman—not flashy like the woman in red—but in a classic, understated way. She had a heart-shaped face, the most beautiful caramel skin I'd ever seen, and stunning gray eyes. Her pixie haircut highlighted sharp cheekbones and a slender neck. She wore a black pantsuit that somehow looked sexy and professional. She'd chewed off her red lipstick and her matching nails were tapping impatiently on the table.

"I've already told everything I know to the detective here," she said. "I'd really like to go home now. It's been an emotional and trying day."

"Miss Taylor is a junior partner at Mr. Sowers' firm," Cole said, sounding like a complete rube.

I almost laughed at the act. She must have gotten on Cole's last nerve for him to go to these lengths to irritate her.

"Just tell the sheriff everything you told me," Cole said.

"Why can't he just read it in your report?" she said, coming to her feet. "I think if you'd like to ask me more questions you can do so at my office. You have my card."

"Where's Bethany Wildes?" Jack asked.

"Who?" Jasmine asked coolly.

Jack smiled. "The woman in the red dress your boss was molesting at the table. Her name is Bethany Wildes. But you know that, so let's move past all of our irritations and just get this done so we can go home."

She narrowed her eyes at Jack and stared at him thoughtfully for a minute. "I don't know where she is. It's only the second time I've met her. I think she lives around here somewhere. Within walking distance."

"Was your boss in the military? Or have any clients that are former military?"

"I wouldn't know," she said. "We all have our

own caseloads. You'd be better off checking with David's secretary."

"You don't seem overly grieved about your friend's death," Jack said.

"Boss," she corrected. "He always invited several of us to meet here on Fridays. And it wasn't just a request. David liked to feel important." She shrugged. "But I've worked hard to be where I am, and I've learned to do whatever you have to do to keep things running smoothly and the money coming in."

"What about cocaine?" Jack asked.

"I don't use drugs," she said.

"But your boss did," Jack said. "Probably a thousand-dollar-a-day habit. Where'd he find Bethany Wildes?"

I could tell she was thrown off guard by the change in direction of the questions.

"Who knows," she said. "Wherever men like David pick up teenagers. He liked them young and goes through them like Kleenex. He would've found another in a couple of weeks to replace her. He always did."

"Could Sowers keep up with a thousand-dollar-a-day coke habit from what y'all bring in at your firm?"

"He's not hurting for cash," she said. "We all

do very well. His drug problem isn't really a secret around the office. His behavior can be unstable, but it hasn't ever affected his work or time in court, so I figure it's none of my business what he puts up his nose. What I have to figure out now is if whatever you drag up on him is going to make the firm look bad enough that I should cut ties."

"Compassion doesn't seem to be one of your strong suits," Jack said.

"Compassion and lawyer don't really go together," she said, rolling her eyes. "At least not if you want to be rich. And I do. Are we done here?"

"For now," Jack said. "Unless Detective Cole has any more questions."

"Oh, not today, sheriff," Cole said. "But I sure look forward to questioning Miss Taylor again soon."

Jasmine didn't bother to acknowledge his comment. Instead she grabbed her handbag and wove her way out of the Purple Pig.

"Interesting group of people," Jack said.

"Oh, yeah," Cole said. "I hate dealing with attorneys."

"Looks like you're going to have to deal with a whole tableful," Jack said. "Follow up with everyone at that table and see what you can find out anything about where Sowers got his drugs."

"What's up with the military angle?" Cole asked.

"Victim was killed by a hollow point .308," Jack said.

"Ahh," Cole said, nodding. "Sniper rifle."

"Martinez and a couple of the guys are out looking for where the shot came from. The drive-by was just cover for the killer. Jaye and I are going to go track down Bethany Wildes."

"Have fun with that," Cole said, slapping Jack on the shoulder as he headed out.

"Oh, and Cole," Jack said, grinning. "Lily was right about the Porsche too. Looks like you and Martinez are going to have to pony up some cash."

"I'll pay her off in other ways," Cole said, winking.

I closed my eyes. "Everyone is way too comfortable sharing the details of their sex lives with us."

"Ease up, Grandma," Jack said. "Let the kids have their fun."

I elbowed Jack in the ribs and headed outside. I could hear his chuckle behind me.

CHAPTER FOUR

JASMINE HAD BEEN RIGHT ABOUT BETHANY LIVING within walking distance. For that matter, Lily had been right about it too.

While I hunted down our coats near our fallen table, Jack did a search for Bethany Wildes in the system and came up with an address just down the block for one of the apartments above all the trendy shops that had been going in recently.

I handed Jack his coat and brushed glass from the back of his collar. "Maybe we should ask Lily the lottery numbers," I said. "Or who's going to win the Super Bowl. Or whether or not Cole is going to propose to her."

"Hmm..." Jack said, helping me with my own

coat. The way he said it made me take a closer look at him. He had his poker face on.

I gasped loudly. "He *is* going to propose to her!"

"Ssh," he said, looking around, but Lily and Sheldon had already left with the body.

"They barely know each other," I whispered.

We moved with purpose around the paramedics and crime scene techs so no one would stop us, and headed south of the courthouse.

"Lily comes from a long line of medicine women," Jack said. "Maybe she knows everything about him already and loves him anyway."

"Good point," I said, chewing my lip. "You think Cole is ready for marriage?"

"Cole is older than I am by a decade. If he's not ready now, he'll never be. Maybe he was just waiting for the right woman."

"I don't know," I said, moving around the blockades the police had put out to keep traffic away from the Towne Square. "I love both of them. But I can't say I have a good feeling about their relationship. They're in that annoying phase of infatuation where they're dancing on clouds and no one leaves dirty socks on the floor. They're blinded by sex."

Jack snorted. "And we don't know what that's like."

"We have a lifetime of friendship behind us. They have twenty years and a whole lot of issues that haven't come to the surface yet between them. Cole's been through some pretty rough things on the job. He's been shot twice. What's she going to do the first time she has to deal with his PTSD? She's just starting her graduate work. How's he going to feel about the time it's going to take her to finish? Or when she has to do a residency two thousand miles away?"

"That's the beauty of it," Jack said. "We're not their parents, and it's not our business. Unless it affects their work."

"We're their friends," I said.

"Yep," Jack said. "And friends let friends make their own choices."

"You must be from an alien planet," I said, shaking my head. "This is Bloody Mary. That is *not* what friends do here. Friends hop right into the mess. You're just scared this one is going to be *really* messy."

Jack cut a glance my direction. "I'm not scared. Just cautious. We've had enough explosions in our life, and more than enough drama. We could use a break."

"That, I agree with," I said, satisfied. "Maybe Cole isn't planning to propose soon. Maybe he just mentioned it in passing as part of his five-year plan."

Jack laughed and put his arm around my shoulder, hugging me close. "I don't know a lot of cops who have five-year plans, but we'll go with that for now. Bethany's apartment is up here on the left."

"Over the candle shop?" I asked. "Good location. I bet it always smells good in her apartment."

"These apartments aren't cheap," Jack said. "And there's a waiting list to purchase. I wonder how she got one."

"How do you know there's a waiting list?" I asked.

"Because we own two of them," he said. "They're both leased and will eventually make a tidy profit."

"No way," I said, stopping in my tracks. "You own two apartments? Why didn't you say anything?"

"Because you told me, and I quote, not to tell you about all the money stuff and that I should just make you sign any financial papers without you having to read it or listen to me talk about it."

"Yeah, yeah," I said. "I remember. I just figure you'd mention something like that in passing."

"I have mentioned it in passing," he said.

"Your eyes usually glaze over and then you try to distract me with food or sex until I change the subject. I've always kind of enjoyed that our money makes you uncomfortable."

I was fighting not to squirm under my coat. It still made me uncomfortable. Which was why I'd learned to distract with food or sex.

"Maybe we can stop by the taco place on the way home," I said. "They stay open late and I never got dessert."

"Are tacos considered dessert food now? Good deflection, by the way."

"I thought I was being subtle," I said.

"I'm not sure subtle is a word I'd use to describe you," he said. "Sometimes a situation calls for a scalpel and sometimes it calls for a hatchet. You're more of a hatchet."

I thought about it for a second, trying to decide if I was going to be insulted, but I didn't really mind the moniker. I tended to be blunt and to the point. I wasn't the kind of person who liked to waste words with flattery or my time with conversation that didn't mean anything.

"Thank you," I said. "I think. And you're a scalpel. I can appreciate that we both bring a unique skill set to the table. You're diplomatic with the living, and I can say what I want in front of the dead without hurting their feelings."

Jack smiled. "Your diplomacy is improving. You didn't punch Janice Van Horn in the face last week when she asked if all the plastic surgery you've had was going to inhibit your ability to get pregnant naturally."

"That's only because I wasn't really sure where her face was," I said, making him laugh. "She's had so many face-lifts her lips are on the back of her head, and they must have used her brain matter for those butt injections she got. If I'd had plastic surgery I wouldn't still have the body of a teenage boy."

Jack squeezed the back of my neck and leaned closer to my ear. "As someone who's touched every inch of your body, I can assure you that you are all woman and look nothing like a teenage boy. We do have that giant mirror in the game room," he said. "I'll be happy to show you what you look like through my eyes."

I cleared my throat and quickened my steps, making him chuckle.

"You can run, but you can't hide," he said, catching up.

"Believe me," I said. "I'm not hiding. But I figure the faster we can do this the sooner I get tacos and mirror sex. Maybe we can still redeem part of our Doug-free weekend."

"I'm sure we can find a few free minutes between murder and tacos."

"Bethany Wildes isn't our tenant, is she?" I asked.

"No," Jack said. "She's next door to one of our units though."

"Handy," I said, and we crossed the street.

The buildings on this block had been old and vacant and in disrepair for at least a decade. They'd originally been two stories of orange brick, and various warehousing and industrial businesses had occupied the space over the years. But some new developer had moved in with a big vision and painted the ugly orange brick white, added a bunch of cedar posts and black hanging gaslights, and added a whole third floor.

There was a private entrance to the residential area at the back of the building through a gated courtyard. Jack punched in the code and the decorative iron gate opened.

"Handy that you know the code," I said. "Now we can surprise her."

"People love surprises," Jack said.

"You keep saying that," I said softly, "But I don't think that's true after a certain age. Surprises can lead to heart attacks or getting punched in the face."

Jack's lips twitched as he opened the back door and we walked up the stairs to the second floor.

"This must be fun to move furniture up and down," I said.

"One of the many reasons we live in a house instead of an apartment," Jack commented. "This is her in 2A."

Jack knocked on the door and we waited several minutes with no response, but I could feel someone on the other side of the door.

Jack knocked again and said, "This is Sheriff Lawson and Dr. Graves. We have a few more questions to ask you about David Sowers," and the door opened quickly.

"Ssh," Bethany said. Her face was red and swollen from crying, and she'd changed out of the red dress and only wore her bathrobe. "I do not want the neighbors to hear. Come in, come in."

I couldn't help my surprise at hearing her thick Slavic accent. And with her face scrubbed free of makeup she looked more child than woman. I was starting to have a bad feeling about all of this.

"Are you Bethany Wildes?" Jack asked.

"Yes," she said, quickly, wrapping her arms protectively around her waist.

Jack nodded. "Maybe we could sit down?" His tone was friendly, and he was trying to put her at ease, but I wasn't sure a woman like Bethany would ever be put at ease by a man.

"We know this has been a difficult night for you," I said gently, taking a step in front of Jack so her focus would be on me. I could see the fear in her eyes. I looked at Jack and said, "Maybe you could get her a bottle of water."

"There..." Bethany swallowed hard. "There is water in kitchen. In refrigerator."

Jack nodded and stepped out of the room, and I saw Bethany visibly give a sigh of relief.

"Your home is beautiful," I said, taking a seat next to her on an overstuffed white couch. The robe dwarfed her and she curled her legs beneath her so only her pale hands and face were visible. She'd obviously showered as her blond hair was still wet and slicked back from her face. Her light gray eyes were large and scared and confused, and seeing her in this moment made me hate David Sowers and the men like him who preyed on the innocent.

It wasn't a large apartment, but the old brick had been painted white and there were exposed wooden beams and industrial-looking pipes on the ceiling. She'd used bright colorful pillows and afghans in blues and greens and golds to soften the harshness of the white.

She looked around as if seeing it for the first time. "Yes," she said.

"How long have you been in America?" I asked.

"Not long," she said. "Few months."

I nodded, understandingly. "What's your real name?"

Her eyes widened and red splotches of color came into her cheeks.

"You're safe now," I told her. "Whatever has happened to you. I want you to know you're safe. Let us help you."

She was silent for a long time, and I didn't think she was going to answer.

"Kateryna," she said.

"It's a beautiful name," I said.

She laughed, but there was no humor in it. "It is cruel joke," she said. "Given to me when I was six by the house mother. I do not remember my name before then. Kateryna means pure. I did not know why they all laughed so hard when they named me. Now I do."

I wasn't sure I could speak if I wanted to. There were some memories that were too painful to share, but I could still see them in her expression. She was a child.

"How old are you?" I asked.

"Eighteen," she said.

"How old were you when you met David Sowers?"

"Fourteen," she said. "He would come to Ukraine on business and request me. And then one day he bought me clothes and told me to pack and he paid the house mother. So I left with him and came here."

Rage like nothing I'd ever felt welled up inside of me, and I worked hard to keep my voice calm and level.

"Did you give a statement to one of the policemen at the restaurant?" I asked.

Her cheeks colored again and she shook her head.

"I escaped out kitchen," she said. "I was good at escaping the house mother. But they always find you. Just like you found me."

"You're safe," I told her again.

"I'm not supposed to talk to police," she said. "Mr. David said police are corrupt and they'll put me in cell if I talk to them. I'm not supposed to talk to anyone. Go anywhere without Mr. David. I show my ID and that is all. No words."

"Let me tell you a little secret," I told her, not bothering to hide the passion in my voice. "Mr. David is a liar and a bad man. He told you that because if the police knew what he was doing to you then he would be the one put in a cell. The police in America will help you. My husband, Jack, is in the kitchen. He is the best man I know. He will help you. *We* will help you."

"I think it is too late to help me," she said.

Her eyes were dry and I wondered if she'd ever been allowed to shed tears.

"It's never too late," I said. "And I know you have no reason to trust me, but I would like for you to talk to Jack like you are talking to me. We are going to find who did this tonight. And we are going to find out more about David Sowers. There could be other girls he's done the same to."

"There are," she said. "My friend Anna. He paid the house mother for her too, and he took her. Will your Jack help me find Anna?"

"Yes," I said, knowing Jack would do everything he could to fulfill a promise I was making on his behalf.

Jack had been listening from the kitchen and he took that moment to come out and take a seat in the farthest seat from Kateryna. I saw her stiffen, and her gaze was one of distrust.

"What David Sowers did to you was wrong," Jack said. "What any of the men did to you was wrong. You were just a child."

Kateryna nodded, but she didn't say anything.

"Did David Sowers live in this apartment with you?" Jack asked.

She shook her head and said, "No. He told me to stay here. I had to always be here when he came or he would be very angry. I took money from his wallet sometimes. I thought if I got enough I could..." She shrugged. "It is stupid."

"No," Jack said. "It's very smart."

"He left on trip and I tried to go to the store to buy food when there was no more, but he was waiting for me when I returned. It was not good. He found out about the money."

"He didn't want the neighbors to see you or for you to talk to people without him," Jack said. "He was afraid you would tell them the truth."

"This is all I have. This is my home. He paid for everything. I have food and nice clothes. I have nothing without him."

"Did you know he was married?" Jack asked.

"No," she said. "He did not talk about that. Just business. Always business. He stayed over every Friday night. Like tonight. But he usually come during the day. Sometimes for breakfast, usually for lunch. He said he was busy man but had needs. Then he would leave until next time. It was really not so bad. He mostly left me alone."

"You speak English well," I said.

She nodded. "The house mother insisted we all learn languages. English, German, Italian. She told us if we could satisfy them well then our station might be elevated. She said it was great honor to be bought."

"We believe someone targeted only David Sowers tonight," Jack said. "Did he ever speak about being in danger or feeling threatened?"

"No," she said. "He was always the one in control. I cannot imagine him being afraid of anyone."

"What about his work?" I asked.

"I do not understand when he talks about work," she said. "He uses big words. But I know he is very important. There is a man. Roger Goodwill I think is his name. There is a trial coming soon."

I wasn't familiar with the name, but I could tell by the look on Jack's face that he was.

"The people you were having dinner with tonight," Jack said. "Do you know them?"

"Not well," she said. "Except for Mr. Kirby. Mr. David has only taken me to restaurant a couple of times. As a reward for obeying."

"Kirby?" Jack asked.

"I do not know his other name," Kateryna said. "Mr. David only told me I must call him

Mr. Kirby. He was with Mr. David when Anna left."

"Oh, was he?" Jack asked, and I could tell things were not going to go well for whoever Mr. Kirby was. "What about the drugs?"

Kateryna pressed her lips together tightly and her wan face managed to lose any remaining color.

"Drugs are bad," she said. "House mother always said that we should not do drugs because that is how you end up dead, and when you are dead no one makes a profit."

"Drugs are bad," Jack agreed. "David Sowers used them."

It wasn't a question.

"Yes," she said. "He want me to do it too, but I told him no. Sometimes I wanted to take them." She looked ashamed, as if she were giving a grave confession. "Sometimes when he took the drugs he would go crazy. And I thought maybe if I took them too then it would not be so bad. Maybe I would not remember."

"You were right not to take them," Jack assured her.

"He always kept some here," she said. "Can you take it? I do not know what to do now that he is gone. What to do with his things."

Jack arched a brow. "He left his things here?"

"Yes," she said. "Come to the bedroom. I will show you." Then she looked back over her shoulder and smiled—the first smile I'd seen from her. "I say that to men before, but it is different this time."

Her humor caught us both off guard and we laughed a little uncomfortably.

"Yes, it is different this time," Jack said.

The bedroom was large and the corner picture windows looked out over the street. I could see the glow from the neon sign at the Purple Pig, as well as part of the park and the courthouse. The bed was as large as a lake, and like the other room everything was all white except for the colorful pillows and afghans. There were no personal pictures. No decorative pieces or jewelry that a woman normally had sitting around.

"These afghans are beautiful," I said, touching one in hues of deepest navy that faded to sky blue.

"Oh." I could tell she was surprised. "Thank you. There is a lot of time to knit while I watch the television. This way," she said, leading us to a large walk-in closet.

The closet was the size of a small bedroom and just off the bathroom. A chandelier hung in the center over a round white cushioned bench.

It was meticulously organized, and there were many pieces of clothing with the tags still on them. There were his and hers shoe shelves that had no empty spaces. I'd always wondered how people had that many shoes when there weren't enough days in the year to wear them all.

All of Kateryna's shoes had red soles and spiked heels. There were no tennis shoes or anything that looked remotely comfortable. Her clothes looked mostly formal or dressy, much like what she'd worn to the bar, and there was a small vanity area in the closet where several different wigs were displayed on head stands.

David Sowers' side of the closet held an array of suits and crisply pressed button-down shirts. There was even a tuxedo in a clear hanging bag.

Kateryna pulled open one of the drawers and there was a small keypad. She typed in a code and the mirror on the wall swung open, revealing a safe.

"He did not think I knew the combination," she said, bitterly. "But there were many times he had too much to drink. Americans do not hold their liquor well. It was not difficult to see the numbers while he was so clumsy."

She opened the mirror fully and typed in the code on the safe.

"He must have been really worried what

might be found in that safe to have this kind of protection," Jack said. "Another good reason to keep you secret."

Kateryna took a step back so Jack could look inside. And then he looked back at me. I still had my medical bag slung across my body and I reached inside for a pair of gloves and a couple of evidence bags.

"Looks like he's got a couple of weeks stocked to feed his habit," Jack said, pulling out a dozen or so vials identical to the one I'd found in Sowers' pocket. "Do you know where he got these?"

Kateryna shook her head. "I do not know. He would sometimes come in with a bag and go straight to the closet. He always had some with him."

"Several prescriptions," Jack said, dumping them in the evidence bag and then handing it to me.

I looked at the labels. "Looks like he's getting the scripts from different doctors. Vicodin. Muscle relaxers. More of the erectile dysfunction meds. None of these with the ED meds go well together. Usually you see a mix of Viagra and meth for the extra stimulation. But cocaine will counteract it, or can even cause cardiac arrest."

"Speak of the devil," Jack said, holding up a

small plastic bag with white powder. "What are you willing to bet he needed the stimulant to counteract his cocaine use so the ED meds worked properly?"

"That's a sucker's bet," I said. "It's amazing this guy was still alive and functioning at the level he was at. I'll know more once I get him on my table, but the body and brain could only sustain that kind of use for so long."

Kateryna shifted back and forth from foot to foot, and clutched her robe. "The little bag of powder. He called it his Friday night special. When he would visit me during the week he would take the little blue pills. But on Friday night he would take the blue pill with the powder in the bag. I did not like Friday nights. Being with him was...different."

"Yes, I can imagine," I said, my anger fueling again.

"There's a locked case in here," Jack said. "Do you know the combination for it?"

Kateryna frowned and looked at the small black case Jack was holding. It was the size of a laptop and about six inches deep.

"I do not know that case," she said. "I have not seen it before."

"When was the last time David came in and went straight to the closet?" Jack asked.

"This morning," she said. "Very early. I was not awake yet. He did not stay. He just let himself in, told me to wear red dress tonight, and then left."

"Thank you for helping us," Jack said. "This might help us find who killed David Sowers."

Her mouth pressed into a thin line and then she said, "I would like to thank the man who did. Mr. David was not good man."

"Do you have any money for food?" Jack asked.

She shook her head, looking terrified all of a sudden. The thought of truly being on her own a reality that was quickly setting in.

"I do not know what to do," she said. "Do I have to leave this place?"

"Not right now," Jack told her. "I'm going to send a nice woman over to bring you some money and other essentials. I'll check with the building to see about the terms of the apartment lease. Do you have a phone?"

"Yes, but I do not know the number," she said, pointing to the black cordless phone on the nightstand. "Mr. David was the only one who knew the number. I had to answer by three rings or he would come over."

"Okay," Jack said. "We'll take care of that too." He handed her a business card. "This is my name and number. Call if you need help or if you think of anything else you can tell us about who might want to hurt David Sowers."

She nodded and followed us to the door, and when we opened it to leave she stood out of the way in case there were neighbors who might see her. Freedom was a concept she'd never experienced.

Neither Jack nor I spoke until we got back down to the street, and he pulled his cell phone out. His jaw was clenched so tight I could see the vein in his neck.

"Who are you calling?" I asked.

"Someone who might be able to give that girl a fighting chance."

CHAPTER FIVE

WHEN I WAS A KID, I'D LIKED TO PRETEND THAT Jack's mom was my own. She'd practically raised me, and she'd never once looked at me as less than because of who my parents had been or because I'd always been a little bit of an outcast. And she'd never once made me feel like I wasn't good enough for her son.

Ruth Lawson was tiny and tough as nails, and I couldn't think of anyone better that Jack could have called to help Kateryna stand on her own two feet.

I listened to Jack explain the situation to his mother, and I could hear her outrage coming through the receiver. I flipped up the collar of my coat since we were walking into the wind, and ducked my head slightly.

I was anxious to get David Sowers on my table and open him up. It must have been pure evil that had kept him alive, because his habits probably should've killed him many times over. I was trying to figure out how to get Jack to drop me off at the lab instead of going home for the night.

By the time Jack had hung up we were almost back to the Purple Pig.

"What did she say?" I asked. "I got the gist from her yelling, but what did she say specifically?"

"She's going to get everything together and come meet with Kateryna first thing in the morning," Jack said. "Mom and Dad have donated time and money to a couple of different trafficking nonprofits, so they'll be a big help. Kateryna was obviously given fake legal documents, but if anyone can move through red tape Mom can. I can only imagine how many other girls there are like Kateryna right under my nose. King George is an easy target because we're isolated. There could be a trafficking nest right under our noses. What is happening to this county?"

"I don't know," I said. "I miss the days when regular murders were the worst we had to deal with. The big city keeps pushing outward, and we're getting sucked in. David Sowers is just one guy, and he had more cocaine on him than I've seen since I started as coroner here. He's also somehow at the center of a sex trafficking ring, but we only know about it because he's dead."

"Not very comforting," Jack said. His steps quickened in his anger, and he shoved his hands in his coat pockets. "People like Sowers come here because they think they can fly under the radar. He can join the KC or the Lion's Club and sponsor a Little League team. I'm sure he pays his country club dues and probably shows up for church every Sunday. But he's still the kind of bastard who will fly to another country and buy an underage girl. And he's just arrogant enough to think he can hide her in plain sight, and that law enforcement in a place like this is too stupid to know what to do about it."

"I personally believe that David Sowers getting a bullet in his head was the easy way out. I know you well. When you take down everyone who is associated with him they're going to all wish for their own bullet by the time you're done with them."

"You're a good egg," Jack said affectionately. "Have I ever told you that?"

"Yes," I said. "But I don't mind hearing it every so often."

The paramedics had packed up shop by the time we returned and everyone had finished giving statements, but Martinez and a few uniforms were still on the street. Martinez hustled over as soon as he saw us.

"Found the shell casing," Martinez said, grinning. He held up the bag for Jack to see.

"Snipers are trained not to leave anything behind," Jack said, eyes narrowing with thought. "Maybe this guy is an amateur and got off a lucky shot."

"I don't know," Martinez said. "But it's a hell of a shot. There's a good clip in the wind tonight, and lots of movement in the periphery. Would've been easy to hit someone else in the crowd."

"Where'd you find the casing?" Jack asked.

"Looks like the shot was taken from the bell tower at the courthouse," Martinez said. "Night security guard let us in, but he said everything was quiet until the shots were fired. No one in and no one out of the building. He has a list of the last employees out of the building. Said everyone usually clears before too late on a Friday. He's making a copy of the log for us."

"Just one security guard on duty?" Jack asked.

"Yeah," Martinez said. "Says he does rounds every hour on the hour, but he's an older guy so I can't see him making those stairs that many times in a night. There are entry points at the front and back, plus a fire escape door on the west side of the building that's accessed through the stairwell. But opening the door triggers the fire alarm. Then there's a second-floor entry from the skywalk that leads to the parking garage, but you've got to have card access to utilize that door and there's a record of who goes in and out."

"We'll need to get a copy of that information," Jack said.

"Already on it," Martinez said. "Someone could've been waiting up there all day until the time was right. The clock tower is closed because of construction, and the door is locked leading to the stairwell. It's not keycard access though. Security guard gave us the key.

"Once we got up there space was a little tight for three of us so Royce hung back on the stairs. It's just an open railing, so plenty of opportunity to fall to your death if you're not paying attention."

I snorted out a laugh and Martinez winked at me.

"It's a construction zone, so plenty of dust. There was some disturbance of dust on the floor, but it was smeared so not sure if the guys can pick up any partial shoe prints. Shooter cut out the pane of glass instead of breaking it."

"Had the equipment with him," Jack said, nodding. "Or maybe hid it up there when he was doing recon. When was the last time the construction crew was up there working?"

"I'll find out," Martinez said. "Night guard didn't know since they're never there while he's on duty."

Jack nodded. "Find anything else?"

"There were a couple of marks on the windowsill where he rested the rifle. It was really just his bad luck and our good fortune about the casing. They removed the floor and laid down plywood and a couple of loose boards for the workers to walk on. There was just the tiniest crack where the casing must have rolled into. Royce actually saw the glint of metal down below while he was on the stairs. I had Royce climb over the rail and risk life and limb for the casing. You don't get to be a detective without a few perks on the job."

"Is Royce still alive?" Jack asked.

"Sure, boss," Martinez said, grinning. "Nothing a little therapy won't clear up. I figure our shooter didn't have time to go down and get it himself. It took the three of us a good fifteen minutes, and Plank and I both had to hold on to Royce to keep him steady. One guy wouldn't have been able to get it by himself."

"That makes more sense," Jack said, nodding. "His bad fortune and our good luck. Good work, Martinez. See if forensics can pull a print from the casing too."

"Sure thing. What's in the case?" he asked, nodding at the black box we'd retrieved from Sowers' closet.

"That's the million-dollar question," Jack said. "It's a regular combination lock. We just need to get it to the station and get it opened up."

We all walked together back inside of the Purple Pig. There were a couple of uniform cops talking to Cole, Alex Denaro, and a birdlike man in a blue parka with a clipboard. His black hair was slicked back and his mustache pencil thin. I was assuming he was the insurance guy, but he could've been an extra in *The Godfather*.

Cole saw us, nodded, and left the uniforms to come over. "We're about finished here," he said. "Crime scene techs are packing up. A couple of our guys told Denaro they'd help him board up his windows." Then he looked down at the case in Jack's hand and the evidence bags and let out a low whistle. "That's a lot of blow. That wasn't all on the victim was it?"

"In a manner of speaking," Jack said. "We found the woman in the red dress. Lily was right again. She has an apartment a block away within walking distance. That's where the victim kept his stash."

"She let you come in and take it?" Cole asked, skeptically.

"Yeah," Jack said, looking down at the evidence haul. "I'm pretty sure we've uncovered a hornet's nest with this one. Turns out the woman is Ukrainian and she's only been in the United States for a few months, but she's known Sowers since she was fourteen. She just turned eighteen and he's got a bill of sale."

"Ah, hell," Cole said, rubbing the back of his neck. "He got her fake documents. That's not easy to do nowadays. Not if she's traveling internationally."

"I don't normally speak ill of the dead," Martinez said, giving the sign of the cross, "but it sounds to me like this guy needed killing."

"I can't say I disagree at this point," I said.

Jack blew out a breath. He was one of those people who believed in the law and that the justice system worked. He believed in fighting for the innocent, and serving those whose lives had been taken senselessly by another.

I understood Jack, and I knew it was a code he had to live by so he could keep doing the things he did day in and day out. He had to believe in the system and that he was making a difference. Otherwise, I'm not sure he could put on the badge every day.

Personally, I was a little more willing to play fast and loose with varying shades of gray. I believed that there were some people in the world who needed killing. But I also believed in Jack. So I'd keep hunting for a killer, even though it looked like he'd done the world a favor.

"We've got a good amount of cocaine and a recreational amount of meth," Jack said, "Both on the victim and in the apartment where he's housing Bethany Wildes, a.k.a. Kateryna. It's enough to get a search warrant for his primary residence and his office. Was next of kin notified?"

"Yeah," Cole said. "A uniform and the chaplain went to tell her. The media got hold of Sowers' name just in time to make the evening news."

"Good," Jack said. "We'll serve the search warrants first thing in the morning. Jasmine Taylor said the whole office knew about his drug habit, so that gives us access at his office. And Kateryna told us Sowers purchased her from a woman she calls the house mother back in Ukraine. Who knows how many girls he's purchased over the years. I want his financials and any other records that might show transactions like that."

"Ooh, boy," Cole said. "You were right about the hornet's nest. I love serving warrants on a den of vipers. I mean, attorneys."

Jack's smile was sharp. "We're just getting started. Jasmine Taylor also mentioned Kateryna wasn't the only young woman that Sowers brought around on their Friday nights. That sounds to me like Sowers' friends knew about his creepy pastime, which makes them accessories. I want everyone who was at that table with David Sowers tonight gotten out of bed and brought in. We can hold them long enough to search his law office before they decide to delete or shred any files. We probably won't find anything," Jack said. "He'd have to be a moron to keep anything there. But it's going to make them all really mad, and it's worth the extra effort."

"Remind me never to get on your bad side," Cole said.

"Kateryna also mentioned a man named Mr. Kirby," I said. "We're not sure if Kirby is first or last name. She said she'd only met the others at the table tonight a couple of times, but she'd met Kirby because he'd traveled with Sowers to Ukraine. He was there when her friend, Anna, was bought."

Cole was checking the list of names of all the statements that had been taken. "I don't see anyone named Kirby here."

"Then he owes us a statement," Jack said. "Track him down. And take your time bringing them in. You know how things slow down when it's time for shift change."

Martinez grinned. "I love this job."

"I hate to be the voice of reason in all of this," I said. "But what about our killer? We still have a murder to solve. That guy could've miscalculated and killed an innocent bystander. And so could the bozo doing the drive-by. Tonight could've been a bloodbath."

"To me," Jack said, "the fact that it wasn't a bloodbath is going to make it a whole lot easier to identify our killer. That's not a skill set your average farmer doing target practice is going to have. My gut says we're looking for military training."

"Hey, sheriff?" Denaro called out. "I got a couple of guys here I think you're going to want to talk to."

Jack passed Cole the black box and the evidence bags we'd collected from the apartment and said, "Let's get everything logged and taken in, and let's get started on the warrants. Use

Judge Stapleton. He hates corrupt attorneys in his courtroom."

"We're on it," Martinez said.

Alex Denaro was an interesting character. He was likeable, but there was something about him I didn't trust. Maybe it was because he had that slick salesman look about him. Or maybe it was because I knew about his ties to the mob. But there was something inside me that warned not to take everything he said at face value.

"How's it going?" Jack asked Denaro.

Denaro shrugged. "You know how these things go. I figure it's going okay for the kind of night it's been. We're all in one piece and Joey Wizard is taking good care of me."

"Joey Wizard?" I asked.

"It's not his last name. Everyone just calls him that cause he's a real wizard in the insurance business. Isn't that right, Joey?" Denaro called out.

Joey Wizard gave a thumbs-up, but didn't look up from his clipboard.

"Good guy, Joey Wizard," Denaro said.

"Looks like it," Jack said. "You wanted us to talk to someone?"

"Yeah, yeah," Denaro said, leading us to a round corner booth. "Over here. These are a couple of my valet boys. Darnell and J.D. They were out parking cars when all the shooting started. They're good boys."

Denaro nodded matter-of-factly and slapped one of them on the shoulder with encouragement. "I'll be back in a second."

"Thanks for sticking around," Jack said. "I'm Sheriff Lawson. This is Dr. Graves. What's going on?"

"It's Bobby," one of the guys said. "He's gone missing."

"What's your name?" Jack asked.

"Oh, umm...I'm Darnell," he said. "Darnell Watkins."

Darnell reminded me of a greyhound—tall and lean with a long nose and oversized ears. His hair was long enough to help cover his ears, and his facial features were an interesting mix of Asian and African American. There was a smattering of freckles across his nose. He was young, early twenties at the most.

"Okay," Jack said. "Who's Bobby?"

"Oh, umm...he's the other valet," Darnell said. "Bobby Pickering."

"What do you mean he's missing?" Jack asked.

Darnell looked at J.D. and then back at us. "Friday nights are pretty crazy, you know? We usually have four valets but Steven called in sick tonight. I don't think he was sick though. He and I worked last night's shift together and he was talking about how he had this big fight with his girlfriend because he was spending all his time working instead of with her. He's trying to save up for an engagement ring, but she don't know that. I'm thinking he called in sick to take his lady out."

"Focus, Darnell," J.D said. "They don't care about all that."

"Right, sorry," Darnell said.

"No problem," Jack said.

"Anyway," Darnell said. "Cars were stacking up and we were all hustling back and forth. We park all the cars at the new garage behind the courthouse. They let us use it on the weekends. All of a sudden, we heard all the gunfire and things were crazy there for a while. It was nuts and there was all this screaming and sirens, but then all the people started wanting their cars when the police were done, so Mr. Denaro told us to get back to work and let's get everyone out of here. He even offered us overtime. He's a pretty cool boss."

"Good grief, Darnell," J.D. said, shaking his head. "Get to the point. I want to go home too. It's after midnight."

J.D. looked to be a few years older than

Darnell. His face had a nice tan considering it was February, and his dark-blond hair was well cut and styled with product on top. He was nice looking with a good build and soft gray eyes.

"Sorry," Darnell said again. "I'm nervous. I've never talked to the cops before."

"Just relax," I told him. "Cops are just people. Mostly."

Darnell laughed nervously. "Yeah, right."

J.D. rolled his eyes. "The last time we saw Bobby was before the shooting started. All three of us were parking cars. We were starting to get backed up, so things were kind of fast and furious. I was just about to leave the parking garage to come get another car when the shooting started."

"Where were you?" Jack asked Darnell.

"I'd just gotten in one of the new Broncos," Darnell said. "Bright yellow. Fully loaded and sweet as they come. I was pulling up to the stop sign on the corner when that black SUV rolled by and opened fire."

"Did you see the shooter?" I asked.

"Nah, the angle was wrong. I couldn't see the driver's side. Just caught the back end."

"I don't understand what this has to do with Bobby," Jack said. "Where was he when the shooting started?"

"I'm not sure," J.D. said, "I thought he was right behind me in the parking garage, but I guess he wasn't. We looked for him, and I was afraid maybe he'd been on the sidewalk and been hit."

"I even tried his cell phone," Darnell said. "Went straight to voicemail."

"Maybe he just went home after he gave his statement," I said.

"That's what we're trying to tell you," Darnell said. "We looked everywhere for him. And we're pretty sure that black SUV the shooter used was parked in the garage. The owner of it came and turned in his claim check, but it was gone from the numbered spot we'd marked on the ticket."

Jack's brows rose in surprise. "Word of advice," he said. "Next time lead off with that information."

"Y'all think Bobby could've been the shooter?" I asked.

Darnell and J.D. looked at each other with concern etched across their faces.

Denaro came back over at that moment with a thin file folder and he handed it to Jack. "Bobby's personnel file," Denaro said. "Not much info in there, but it's all the paperwork he filled out when I hired him. We only valet Thursday through Sunday, so all these guys have other jobs during the week. Bobby was no different.

"What was his daytime job?" Jack asked.

"Contracting," J.D. said. "He's a painter. Works for Miller Construction. They're the ones putting up that new subdivision over on Reformation Street."

"Thanks," Jack said to Denaro. "This saves me a lot of time."

"I heard what you were saying to that other cop earlier," Denaro said. "You're gonna want to read what's in there. Told you it wasn't my family. Here's the list, by the way." He took out a folded piece of paper from his shirt pocket and handed it to Jack.

Jack put the paper in his pocket and opened the personnel file, scanning the pages quickly. And then he looked up in surprise. "Bobby was a veteran?"

"One of the reasons I hired him," Denaro said. "I like hiring veterans when I can. He seemed like a good kid, so I don't want to make assumptions about anything that might be a coincidence. But I'd feel better if maybe someone swung by his place and made sure he was okay. Maybe he just got freaked out by the gunfire and took off. PTSD or something."

"Yeah," Jack said. "We'll swing by and do a welfare check."

"I'd appreciate it," Denaro said. "You boys go on home if the sheriff is done with you. I'm sure your women are worried and will want to show you their appreciation that you're still alive."

"You don't have to tell me twice," J.D. said, scooting out of the booth.

Darnell sighed, looking terribly forlorn. "I'm in between ladies at the moment. And I really needed this job. I'm saving for my own place. I'm gonna have to find another restaurant I can pick up some shifts."

Denaro slapped Darnell on the back good-naturedly. "We'll be back up and running in a couple weeks. I've got Joey Wizard and a top-notch construction crew. You don't grow up like I did and not have a crew in your back pocket. We'll be back in business in no time. You boys take a couple of weeks off and do what young people do. Work will be here when you come back. Isn't that right, sheriff?"

Jack nodded and said, "Thanks again for the file." And then we headed out of the Purple Pig for the final time that night.

CHAPTER SIX

Since Lily and Sheldon had taken the Suburban when they'd transported the body, Jack and I were left with his Tahoe. As soon as we got in the vehicle Jack called Cole.

"Cole," Jack said. "Do you have a Bobby Pickering on your list of statements that were given?"

"Hang on a sec and let me check," Cole said.

I could hear the shuffling of papers along with the squeaky desk chair Cole refused to get rid of. He said the chair fit him like a glove and annoyed his desk mate at the same time, so it was a win all around.

"I don't have a Pickering on the list," Cole said.

"Thanks," Jack said. "Can you send someone out to do a welfare check? He's one of the valets at the Purple Pig. His co-workers said the last time they saw him was before the shooting started, and then he disappeared. He's got military training. I've got his personnel file from Denaro, but let's go ahead and run a full background check."

"I'll take care of it," Cole said. "We're a little thin right now, and we got a call for an armed robbery over at the Shell station in King George."

"Anyone hurt?" Jack asked.

"Shots were fired at officers, but everyone is okay," Cole said. "They're bringing the suspects in now."

Jack looked at me. "Things are going to be crowded at the station tonight."

"Makes things more interesting," Cole said. "Beats the heck out of a slow night."

"I'll be in as soon as I drop Jaye off," Jack said and disconnected.

"No need to take me all the way home," I said. "Just drop me at the lab. I'm itching to get started on Sowers. I can drive myself home when I'm finished with the autopsy."

"You just don't like going to bed without me," Jack said, giving me a wink.

"That's true too," I said. "Who else am I going to put my cold feet on?"

"Ahh," he said. "Marriage is the gift that

keeps on giving. Single men don't know what they're missing."

I laughed and rolled my eyes. "Consider yourself lucky you came to your senses when you did. What are your thoughts on Bobby Pickering? You think he could've been the shooter?"

Jack shrugged. "I've never believed in coincidences. The fact that he's missing and has a military record definitely makes him a person of interest. We just have to find him first."

It was a short ride to the funeral home since it was only a couple of blocks from the Towne Square, and we turned onto Catherine of Aragon, which was one of the oldest streets in Bloody Mary. There was a mix of small brick shotgun houses that were a couple of hundred years old, a few craftsman-style houses built during an architectural revival at the turn of the twentieth century, and then there was the funeral home, which was a three-story Colonial that didn't really fit in with anything and took up two full lots. Across the street from the funeral home was a strip mall built in the eighties that was an eyesore and everyone hated, but someone had recently bought the space and updated it so it looked like Chip and Joanna Gaines had waved their Magnolia wands at it. Somehow that was enough to get businesses in there that were actually turning a profit.

"How you doing?" Jack asked. "You never got your dessert. You gonna make it?"

"I'll make do," I said, already thinking about the Hostess snacks I had hidden in the pantry at the funeral home. "Thanks for loving me. I know I can be extra."

"It's the extra parts I love the most," Jack said. "You're extra generous even though you don't want people to think you are. And you're extra kind to those who are hurting. And you've loved me extra since we were kids. I love the extra."

I cleared my throat uncomfortably and blinked the tears away. "Wow," I said, my voice husky. "I was not expecting that. You are so going to get lucky the next chance I have."

Jack pulled the Tahoe up under the covered portico and gave me a kiss. "If I didn't need to be at the station half an hour ago you'd already be naked."

I snorted a laugh and opened the door to hop out of the Tahoe. I could tell his mind was already on what was waiting for him at the station. I didn't take it personally. My mind was already on David Sowers.

"Text me before you head home," he said.

"Will do. Love you."

Jack waited until I was safely inside and had the door locked behind me and the alarm set, and then I saw his headlights disappear down the driveway. Most people might be put off by being in a funeral home with a dead body in the middle of the night. It had never bothered me. In fact, I'd always welcomed the quiet that came with being completely alone.

My grandparents had built the Colonial and had lived on the top two floors while running the business on the ground floor. Unfortunately, my grandmother had died under mysterious circumstances when she'd fallen from a third-story window. Supposedly, she and my grandfather had been having some issues—most notably the mistress he'd been sneaking into their bed and the money he'd been stealing from the funeral home to run away with her.

The scandal hadn't destroyed the business, but it was decided the best course of action was for my parents to take over after Grandmother's funeral and Grandfather's elopement to the new Grandma Graves. But my parents had their own scandal to deal with, and it almost had been too much for the business to survive. I'd spent a lot of time researching the Graves family tree, and it seemed anyone with Graves blood coursing through their veins had a proclivity for criminal activity. You can't imagine how thrilled I was to find out that Graves blood didn't actually course through my veins.

I stopped to make a pot of coffee, and then I opened the pantry and used the step stool to reach the Hostess cinnamon rolls I'd hidden on the top shelf.

"Gotcha!" I said, stretching my fingers as far as I could until I touched the corner of the box and could nudge it forward.

The sound of crinkling plastic was music to my ears, and once I had my prize in hand I shoved the box back into hiding. Treats had a way of disappearing in this place. Lily said it was the ghosts of the dead who darkened our doorway, but I was pretty sure it was just me. I'd been blessed with great metabolism, and I'd learned how to survive on vending machine food and burnt coffee during my residency. Doctors typically had terrible eating and health habits. I was almost afraid to change at this point in my life. I was mostly held together with caffeine and gluten.

Once I had the essentials, I typed in the code that opened the lab door. When my parents decided to pursue lawlessness, they did it the right way and made sure everything was top of the line. I had one of the top labs in the state.

There was a soft click and a release of pressure as the door unsealed, and I immediately felt the change in temperature as I crossed the threshold. I debated on whether to use the lift or the stairs since my hands were full, and I decided on the stairs since I needed to counteract my upcoming calorie intake.

I enjoyed the monotony of the routine—the bright white lights and the sound of my soles hitting the metal stairs as I made my way down. No matter how good the ventilation system, there was always the faint smell of antiseptic and embalming fluid. It was the one smell Jack couldn't stomach. He'd take a decayed body any day over chemicals.

I blew on my coffee and took a bite of cinnamon roll while I scrolled through my music library. I was feeling Rat Packish tonight, so I turned it on random and Dean Martin's "Hey Mambo" blared through the speakers.

The sugar and caffeine finally hit my system, so I washed my hands, got a blank autopsy form from the drawer, and attached it to my clipboard. Technology had taken over many parts of the pathology industry, but there was something to be said for doing things with pencil and paper. You could look at x-rays and scans all day, but sometimes you had to touch and see for yourself.

I put on my lab coat and a thick apron, and I went to get David Sowers out of the cooler. I was humming along to Dean by the time I got him out of the bag and had removed all his clothes, and I was tapping my toe to Frank Sinatra by the time I'd scrubbed him down with antiseptic.

I checked all of his pockets again and the hems of his pants, and I found another vial of cocaine sewn into the cuff of his pants. This guy had a serious problem, but I was starting to wonder if he was a social user. Guys like Sowers typically ran in circles of people who had similar habits and income levels. Maybe he carried the extra for other people. It was definitely something to check out. The rats would start coming out of the woodwork once we started digging a little deeper.

There was no beauty in death. For David Sowers—educated, wealthy, and the ability to have anything he wanted at the snap of his fingers—he was still subjected to the humiliation of being nothing more than flesh and bone laid out on a cold metal table.

I turned the music off and turned on my recorder.

"Victim identified through driver's license as David Sowers, age sixty-one. Caucasian male. Hair gray. Eyes blue. Height approximately one hundred and eighty-two centimeters. Weight is eighty-one point six kilograms."

I moved the light closer to the body and photographed every inch of him, looking for distinguishing marks for identification or any other avenues for drug use as I went along.

"Apparent cause of death is GSW to the head," I continued. "Indication of piercing in left ear. Significant swelling in nasal passages. Assumption due to cocaine found on victim at time of death. No sign of linear track marks in arms or between toes to indicate other avenues of drug use."

I took x-rays and then displayed them on my light screen, seeing a picture of David Sowers' life through his bones.

"Remodeled fractures on the metacarpals," I said, furrowing my brow. "Less than a year old. Similar remodeled fractures on ribs two through four. Got in a fight with someone, didn't you?"

I notated the breaks on paper. All in all, David Sowers appeared to be a typical sixty-one-year-old man. He wasn't overweight, though there wasn't any indication he took care of himself physically.

"Let's see what your insides have to say," I said.

I turned the music back on and took blood

and urine samples, along with vitreous fluid from the eye. I could run basic toxicology tests here in the lab, but I'd have to send everything off to the state lab for corroboration and for more in-depth testing since I knew there was likely to be an interesting concoction in Sowers' bloodstream.

Once I took care of the toxicology report I prepped him for his first Y-cut. The music had switched to Sammy Davis Jr. and I hummed along quietly as I made the cut all the way down to the pubic bone. I used shears to peel back skin and muscle and expose the rib cage.

"The candyman can..."

I put the shears back on the tray and grabbed my goggles and the bone saw, the grinding whir dampening the sound of the music as I cut through the rib cage. The way the human body was put together never ceased to amaze me. When the last cut was made, I lifted the rib cage out and had my first look at David Sowers' internal organs. They were not what I would call healthy at first glance.

I reached for the syringe on the tray and drew another blood sample directly from the heart this time, and then I went through the painstaking process of removing each of his organs and weighing them. His heart was enlarged and several arteries that had blockages. His liver was fatty and his lungs indicated he was a smoker or had recently been within the last few years.

Another interesting find was that David Sowers had a prosthetic testicle. We'd have to locate medical records for the reason, but it had been surgically removed for whatever reason and replaced with a prosthetic for symmetry.

I moved on to the skull and removed what was left of his brain. I found several bullet fragments and carefully removed and bagged them to go with the other evidence. By the time I got everything put back in place and sewed up it was almost four, and my coffee and cinnamon roll were wearing off. I rolled him back into the cooler, finished the paperwork, and put the extra samples in the fridge to be sent to the state lab.

I texted Jack to let him know I was finished, and I debated just catching a couple of hours sleep in my office instead of making the drive home. I was just about to text Jack to let him know, but my phone rang.

"I'm out front," Jack said. "I'll follow you home since I'm sure whatever sugar concoction you ate has made you sleepy."

"Hey, it kept me awake while I was operating

power tools," I said, making my way up the stairs and locking the lab door behind me.

"You're right," he said. "It's more important that you keep all your appendages. I'll make sure you're stocked with Hostess CupCakes for life."

I narrowed my eyes and corrected him. "Close," I said. "Cinnamon rolls. How'd you know?"

"I'm a cop. I know everything."

I put on my coat and scarf, and grabbed my bag off the hook. I was too tired to mess with gloves. The cold air stung my cheeks and I said, "If we don't get warmer weather soon I'm going to have to leave you and retire south. This has been the longest winter ever."

Jack flashed his lights at me so I'd see him and I waved. "I'd just follow you. Anytime you're ready to leave just say the word."

"Well, technically we could have been somewhere warm this weekend but you wanted to go to the Purple Pig."

"I feel like we've already had this conversation," he said.

"Just thought it was worth mentioning again."

I hauled myself into the Suburban, trying to display the appropriate amount of energy to prove him wrong about the sugar crash. But my attempt proved to be in vain when my foot slipped on the running board and I half fell into my seat.

"You all right there?" Jack asked, laughter in his voice.

"Hush," I said. "It was slick."

"It's completely dry outside."

"Didn't I tell you to hush? I don't need this kind of negativity in my life." I started the car and plugged in my phone so Jack came through on the speaker. I backed out of the drive and then turned onto Anne Boleyn for the twenty-minute drive home.

"So do you want to know what I found out about Sowers or do you want to keep busting my chops?" I asked.

"Why can't both be an option?" Jack asked.

"I'm too tired to answer that," I said. "My eyes feel fuzzy."

"That's a shame," he said. "I find I'm full of energy. I was hoping you'd help me with that."

"I think you're out of luck," I said. "That part of my body went to sleep a long time ago."

"That sounds like a challenge to me," he said, laughing.

"You're in much too good of a mood," I said. "Things must have gone well at the station."

"I'll let you change the subject for now," he said. "But I'm onto you."

I smiled and squinted my eyes to see the road better. "No doubt. When did this road get so narrow? The Suburban barely fits."

"That's because you're driving in the ditch. There's a bridge coming up so you probably want to fix that."

"Oh," I said, and brought the Suburban back to the middle of the road so I could drive over the narrow bridge that brought us over Machodoc Creek. "Thanks for that."

"Anytime," Jack said. "We've got everyone who was at dinner with the victim in holding for the time being. We'll start interviews at six, so I've only got a couple of hours."

"Then you need to spend it sleeping instead of trying to wake up my sleepy parts."

"I've never needed much sleep," he said, his voice husky.

"Crazy how opposites attract like that," I said.

"All right, all right," he said. "We'll go straight to bed."

"Sleep," I corrected.

"That's what I said."

I could hear the smile in his voice, and I stopped at the sign on the corner of Heresy Road. We were almost home.

"Toxicology report showed the victim's blood alcohol was well over the legal limit," I said. "Narcotics and opiates in the system as well. I've got everything ready to go to the state crime lab to narrow down the sources."

"Pretty much like we figured," Jack said. "Anything unusual?"

"He had a prosthetic testicle."

Jack laughed. "That is unusual, but not really what I was looking for."

"Oh," I said. "He had remodeling on the metacarpals of his right hand and on a couple of ribs. Less than a year old and most likely occurred at the same time."

"Fight?" Jack asked.

"If it was he was on the losing end," I said. "No breaks in the knuckles or defensive fractures. Something came down hard enough on the top of his hand to break all the bones there."

"Ouch," Jack said. "What would do that?"

"I've seen it a couple of times before," I said. "Because of the evenness of the breaks across the top of the hand I'd say it's most likely his hand was stepped on. Nothing else stood out. Other than the hole in his forehead and his brains looked like oatmeal."

"You've always had a way with words," Jack said.

"Maybe I should've been a writer instead of a

doctor. I could see myself as an eccentric recluse."

"You hide away with dead bodies for hours on end. I think you're already there."

"I'm not hiding away," I said. "I'm working."

I stopped in front of our gate and pressed the button on the remote and waited for it to swing open. We'd updated our security significantly over the last year. The gravel crunched beneath my tires as I sped up the driveway, and I'd never been more glad to see the soft glow of lights from the house.

"Guess what?" I asked as I put the Suburban in park under the covered portico that connected the house to the garage where Jack housed all his toys.

The tone of my voice must have given me away because Jack laughed before he answered.

"What's that?

"I think a certain part of me is getting a second wind."

CHAPTER SEVEN

My alarm went off at eight the next morning, and I rolled to my back, reaching my arm across cool sheets to the empty space beside me. I vaguely remembered Jack's alarm going off, but I didn't remember him leaving. He'd gone early to make sure there were no issues with the warrant being served at the law office.

I lay in bed and squenched my eyes closed, trying to will myself back to sleep until my second alarm went off, but it was no use. I was awake. Morning sun shone through the branches of the towering trees outside our bedroom window and a perfect beam of light was bouncing off my forehead. Having a bedroom on the third floor was a little like sleeping in a tree-house except our thread count was higher.

I rolled over once for good measure and pulled Jack's pillow on top of my head, but when I could no longer breathe I gave up and got out of bed. I padded my way to the bathroom and thought about showering, but instead ended up devising a plan for the rest of my Saturday morning while I brushed my teeth.

I needed sleep. Jack had made sure I hadn't had much once he'd gotten his hands on me, and the bags under my eyes were testament to that. I wasn't even sure how he was functioning, but he'd always been kind of superhuman. I would go downstairs, make coffee, and then curl up on the couch in the den where the shades were drawn and it was nice and dark. I could watch a serial killer documentary, nap comfortably, and I didn't have to think about the bed being empty beside me.

I put on a headband and slapped on a green face mask, figuring it would help with the bags, and I put on my thick robe and slippers.

It had been a long time since I'd had the house solely to myself. Having a teenage boy living with us had definitely changed the dynamics of our day-to-day lives. I wasn't quite sure what to do with myself now that the autopsy was finished and I didn't have any other pressing work.

I thought briefly about doing laundry, but didn't want to waste my free time doing something I hated. I wasn't good at resting. It made me uncomfortable. I'm sure that probably said something about me on a deeper level than I was willing to go without a caffeine boost, so I hastened my steps to the kitchen and decided to think about what came next later.

Somewhere between the second floor and the kitchen I'd decided to go all out and use the fancy machine Jack had bought with the flavored espresso and foamy milk that went on top. That seemed like a good decision for a Saturday morning with little sleep.

I stumbled into the kitchen and noticed the note on the coffeepot.

"Will come back to get you as soon as I can to interview Sowers' widow," I read aloud. "Will be at least a couple of hours. I love you. Get some rest. PS The instructions for the espresso machine are taped to the side for you."

My mouth dropped open and I moved over to the espresso machine. And there were the instructions printed neatly in Jack's handwriting.

"He always knows," I said, shaking my head.

I wasn't sure how long I stood there before I felt the presence of someone else in the room. I used my periphery to look for the closest weapon, but unless I wanted to throw the machine itself I was out of luck. Whoever it was would have my throat slit before I could pick it up.

"It's truly exhausting watching you think," a familiar voice said.

I gasped and turned around. And then I launched myself across the room at the man sitting in what looked like the love child of a go-kart and a scooter from the future.

"Where have you been!" I scolded Carver. "Where are Michelle and the girls? We've been so worried about you. What is this ridiculous contraption you're riding? You look like an extra in *Tron*."

Carver laughed in his usual good humor, but I could see the strain around his eyes. And then he got a good look at me.

"Wow," he said. "Terrifying. Is that your natural skin color? Is this the reason you've never invited me over for breakfast before?"

I rolled my eyes and took a step back to really look at him. The last year had taken its toll on Carver. As long as I'd known him, he'd always been somewhat autonomous in his position at the FBI. Only a select few outranked him, and I knew for a fact there were times he only answered to the president. His brain was a commodity the government wanted to make sure didn't fall into the wrong hands—they were in awe of his abilities as much as they feared them. The fact that Carver was one of the best men I knew was the only thing that gave him the freedom it did.

But something was going on that he hadn't confided in us about. We'd had the feeling he'd been keeping secrets, and things had amplified after he'd started digging deeper into Floyd Parker and some of the developers that wanted a piece of King George county. Someone hadn't wanted Jack re-elected as sheriff, and things had gotten dirty, even to the point of an article in the paper about the woman Jack had gotten pregnant when he'd been a teenager.

Carver had done a lot of deep digging to find out about who could've been behind having that kind of information. And whatever he'd found out had changed him. He'd moved his family suddenly from DC to Bloody Mary. It was obvious Carver was scared for his family, and a place like Bloody Mary made it very easy to know if you were being watched or followed by strangers.

But Carver and his wife Michelle had barely been moved into their house when they'd all disappeared. The next thing we knew was the

FBI had raided their house, and they weren't sharing with local law enforcement why. We'd only gotten one message from Carver letting us know he was okay, and that we were supposed to hold on to his computer Magnolia.

Carver in hiding couldn't have been easy, and I couldn't imagine he was doing it alone. Because of my father, he'd almost died and had been wheelchair bound the last several months. He would probably walk again, but not anytime soon.

"Does Jack know you're here?" I asked. And then I paused in thought. "Never mind. Of course he knows you're here. How long do we have before the FBI busts down our door?"

"Thank God you didn't figure out how to use the espresso machine," Carver said. "I'm already exhausted by your questions and you haven't even had coffee yet."

"Oh, excuse me," I said sarcastically. "Maybe I've been worried. But now that I see you're okay maybe I should just punch you for scaring the daylights out of us."

"Just don't punch me in the face," Carver said. "Michelle and Magnolia are both partial to my good looks."

I sighed and shook my head. "At least you named your wife before your cyber girlfriend.

That's progress in the right direction. Are you going to explain what's going on, or are you just here to help me make coffee?"

"I'm going to take that as an invitation to stay," Carver said, and rolled his new chair across the kitchen to the espresso machine. "You like the chair?"

"I'm still trying to process," I said. "It's very fluid. Like it's part of your body."

I hadn't been kidding when I'd said he looked like an extra from *Tron*. It resembled a motorcycle, but the wheels were perfectly spherical so they could move in any direction. They even rose and lowered so it looked almost like he was standing on the tips of his toes to reach the coffee mugs in the cabinet.

"Just a little AI experiment," he said, smiling sheepishly. "She's still getting to know me, but I feel like we're making good progress. Now if only every woman could read a man's mind like Margarite."

"You're going to eventually run out of *M* names to call all of your robot women," I said. "But I like the red. Very stylish."

"Margarite is French," he said. "She'd accept nothing less."

"Does she talk to you like Magnolia?" I asked, the scientist in me curious, even though Carver's

AI experiments were a little too real for my comfort.

Magnolia was Carver's computer. She did everything except have a physical body, and even at times I wasn't so sure. I wouldn't have been at all surprised if Magnolia invaded some poor woman and she showed up on our doorstep one day to make an honest man out of Carver. Of course, she'd have to kill Carver's wife, which was nothing less than I'd expect from a superbot that would probably take over the world someday.

"In a way," he said. "She can hear my voice and respond if I want her to. I injected a transmitter in the back of my neck and she's learning to respond to brain commands."

"I'm pretty sure a lot of superhero stories gone wrong start out like that," I said, getting the milk from the fridge and bringing it to him.

He chuckled and the smell of strong coffee permeated the air. "Now that I'm on a hiatus from physical therapy Margarite has taken over that role. I'm using the muscles in my own legs to stand if I need to reach something out of the way, but she knows exactly how much support to give so I still build strength but don't fall."

"That'll be a big help to a lot of people," I said.

"Yeah, except the market will outprice itself

like it always does and no one will be able to afford it. And then the insurance companies will get involved and make billions. It's the way of things. No one really gets helped in this country without an ulterior motive."

"Wow," I said. "You've grown in cynicism over the last few months. You're starting to sound like me."

"Yeah, well, I've started to see things in a different light recently." He poured the milk into a little black cylinder and pressed the on button. "I've not shared anything with you and Jack for a reason. They're watching and researching anyone connected with me. All I can tell you is that it was not in their plans for Jack to win another term as sheriff. King George's positioning is ripe for development and land deals and there are a few people a lot higher up than me who have been secretly purchasing land and working with lobbyists and developers who just lost out on a whole lot of money and power. They bought Floyd Parker. He was who they needed. Jack has too much local influence and money to meet their needs."

Floyd Parker had been the bane of my existence since my second year in medical school. I'd had one night of bad judgment with him, and he'd never let me forget it, ramping up his torment over the years. Last November he'd decided to run against Jack in the election for sheriff, but when Floyd had killed a man in a hit-and-run accident, not even he could've spun that in his favor.

"So why are you the one on the run instead of me and Jack?" I asked, pouring the foamy milk on top of our coffees.

I carried our drinks over to the breakfast nook and slid into the bench. I remembered there'd been a time not too long ago when I'd sat across from Carver's wife over a different matter.

"Because while I was digging into Floyd Parker and the development deals for the prisons I ended up going down a rabbit hole I couldn't get out of. I'm talking murder and money, and prominent names to go along with it. Some of whom I work for. Or worked for. It's all a bit hazy at the moment on whether or not I have a job. Let's just say that the FBI has become the most distrusted law enforcement agency over the last decade or so for a reason. But I've got some connections, and if I can stay alive long enough I might just see justice done."

"If you stay alive long enough?" I asked. "Where are Michelle and the girls?"

"They're safe," he said. "I can't tell you more than that. And I believe you and Jack are safe too.

Just keep doing what you're doing, and don't talk about me outside of these walls. I've got you protected so no one can see or hear as long as you're inside the house."

"If we're being watched how did you get in here and how are you going to get out?" I asked.

Carver smiled. "I'm a magician," he said. "I have my ways."

I heard the front door open and my heart stopped in my chest. I was halfway standing, not having a clue what I would do if the FBI stormed in.

"Whoa," Jack said, stopping at the kitchen threshold, his eyes wide. "I did not leave you looking like Shrek."

Carver snorted out a laugh and Jack came over to kiss me hello. He slapped Carver casually on the shoulder and then went to make himself a cup of coffee.

"You were keeping this from me," I said to Jack, my fists bunched at my waist. "You are not at all surprised to see Carver here."

"Yes," Jack admitted. "But to be fair, I haven't been keeping it from you that long. I was just as surprised as you when I walked into the kitchen this morning and saw him sitting there. I think we need to upgrade our security."

"I designed your security," Carver said,

waving away the concern. "No one else can get in without your knowledge. Not even Doug."

"That makes me feel so much safer to know that not even a teenager can get past our security," I said dryly.

"Well, in my defense," Carver said. "I had to let myself in. You guys were pretty busy with the whole drive-by thing at the Purple Pig. Weird name for a restaurant, but I liked the look of their appetizers when I Googled the menu. I was going to let you know I was here when you came in last night, but I heard a lot of things that made me pretty uncomfortable and kind of tingly too, so I decided it was best to give y'all privacy."

I felt the heat rise in my face, and I was thankful for the green mask.

"How you've managed to keep that face so pretty all these years will always be a mystery," Jack said, shaking his head.

Carver grinned. "It's my charm. I can get away with almost anything. Unless it's with my wife. Or apparently the FBI. Anyway, I figured I could get in here, get Magnolia, and get a little sleep too. Y'all have comfortable beds. I told Michelle we needed to get beds like y'all's but she said she didn't want to spend the money until she knows we're not going to die."

"Very practical," Jack said dryly. "Do you

know how many agents are watching this house right now? How do you plan to get out of here?"

"Wait, agents are watching this house right now?" I asked, looking back and forth between them. And then I narrowed my eyes at Jack. "Didn't we have a conversation recently about communicating? The last time you didn't communicate with me I found out about a long-lost son."

"Yeah, that was definitely your bad," Carver said, shaking his head at Jack. "Communication is key."

"I appreciate the marriage help," Jack said, giving Carver a thin smile. But Carver sat there innocently looking completely unrepentant. "I've been gathering information the last three days," Jack said, looking at me. "I would have told you once I had some answers. I just haven't gotten any answers yet. I have no idea what's going on in my own town, and now I find out we have someone with Mafia ties and a lawyer involved in sex trafficking all in the same day."

"The world really is going to hell in a hand-basket," Carver said. "Don't beat yourself up. You're not Superman. There will always be evil in the world, despite all the people who feel like love and hugs will make everything better. Good and evil have existed since the beginning of the world. I mean, there were literally four people on the planet and Cain killed Abel. That's a twenty-five percent murder rate. You're doing a lot better than that."

Jack snorted out a laugh and said, "Gee, thanks."

"Don't worry about the agents here in town," Carver said. "They're idiots. I could outmaneuver them in a wheelchair. Oh, wait..." he said, grinning. "You'll know when they send in the big guns. They're assessing the situation. I wouldn't be surprised if anything popping up on your crime radar right now are purposeful distractions. Like I said, we're talking billions of dollars and depraved criminals that rule different parts of the world. And they've all put a target on King George County. It's prime real estate."

"Do you really think the FBI would kill you?" I asked Carver.

"Of course not," he said. "But they'd hire someone else to do it. They like to keep their noses clean of such things. Believe me, there's a whole expense account for dirty work like that. I wouldn't have come at all, but I need Magnolia. She's the only person who can help me."

I'd normally have made a joke about how Magnolia wasn't actually a person, but I could see the gravity in Carver's eyes.

"I've got her locked in the safe," Jack said.

"I know," Carver said, winking. "But I figured I'd let you do the honors of retrieving her for me since this is your house."

"Always a pleasure having you stop by, Carver," Jack said good-naturedly. "When are you leaving?"

Carver just smiled. "You won't even know when I leave. Like I said, I'm a magician."

CHAPTER EIGHT

WHILE JACK WENT TO GET MAGNOLIA FOR Carver, I took the opportunity to run back upstairs and take a quick shower so I didn't scare the next person to walk in the door.

I was in and out in ten minutes and spent another four drying my hair. The sun was out today and not a cloud in sight, so I opted for jeans, a black turtleneck, and a beige suede blazer, along with low-heeled black booties.

I wasn't much of a makeup wearer on my best days, and I figured it would defeat the purpose of the green mask altogether, so I slapped on some moisturizer and called it done.

I'd expected Carver to be gone when I'd come downstairs, so I was surprised to see him still sitting at the table with a plate of fried eggs and bacon and talking to his computer.

"Magnolia, darling," he coaxed. "I didn't mean to stay away so long. I told you bad people are after me. Don't you have any compassion or concern for my safety?"

"You missed our date," Magnolia said, her Southern accent clipped short.

I raised my brows at Carver and his cheeks turned pink. "What kind of date?" I asked.

"Hello, Dr. Graves," Magnolia said. "So lovely to see you again. You have a certain glow about you."

"I just did one of those masks," I said conversationally. "Like a mini spa day without the massage."

"You got the massage last night," Jack said, bringing a plate for me to the table and winking.

"Hubba, hubba," Magnolia drawled. "Now that's what I'm talking about. I bet you never miss a date do you, sheriff? I love movies. Maybe you could watch one with me some time."

"I don't think Jack likes the same kind of movies you do," Carver said, perturbed. "And I told you I had to hide out for a few days until it was safe. And I had to make sure Michelle and the girls were safe. If you don't show some compassion I'm going to have to mess with your programming."

"Fine, fine," she said. "You can make it up to me later. Would you like a rundown of world events and the financial reports while you enjoy your breakfast? That looks delicious by the way, though I must warn you to watch your cholesterol. It was a little high at your last physical."

"I appreciate the reminder," Carver said. "Remember how we talked about keeping certain things private?"

"Yes," Magnolia said in such a way that had me bursting with laughter.

I scooted down the bench across from Carver and Jack sat next to me with his own breakfast and a thick file folder.

"What's all that?" I asked.

"Cursory backgrounds on the victim and his tablemates," Jack said. "And a background on Bobby Pickering. Welfare check came up empty last night. Rents a small two-bedroom house over in Nottingham. Not a great area of town. No one was home and his truck was found on the top floor of the parking garage. A twenty-year-old white Ford F-150. We impounded it and found a .9mm in the glove box and a 32-round magazine under the front seat that would fit nicely in the kind of weapon used during the drive-by. Needless to say, Pickering is a person of interest and wanted for questioning."

"Solid military record," Carver said, turning Magnolia so we could see her screen. "Enlisted in the marines at eighteen in 2011. He's got classified files that I could get into for you, but I'd have to be delicate and it would take a little time. Joined Force RECON in 2014 and did three different tours as part of the War on Terror in Afghanistan, Yemen, and Iraq. Decorated with an honorable discharge about six months ago. No family in the area, but employment is listed as Miller Construction."

"That adds up with what the valets told us," Jack said. "Though the Force RECON information is interesting. He'd certainly have a sniper buddy who could make a shot like that. But we need to find the tie between Pickering and Sowers."

"Maybe Pickering was a client," I said.

"We brought in all of Sowers' electronics and files when we served the warrant this morning," Jack said. "I'll have Cole do a search and see if the name pops."

"How did that go, by the way?" I asked.

"About like you'd expect," Jack said. "It's Saturday so the office was closed. But strangely enough there were two law clerks inside shredding documents. We were able to obtain everything they didn't shred, but we'll never know what was destroyed. Those shredders make it impossible to put the pieces back together again. Cole and Martinez are trying to sift through the files right now, and see what was so important they had to destroy."

"Any drugs?"

"Nope," Jack said. "Place was clean as a whistle. We took Sowers' electronics and files, but the law clerks had clearly had instruction from someone."

"The people he was having dinner with last night?" I asked.

"I'm pretty sure I can be a little more specific than that," Jack said. "We brought in Mr. Kirby. Guess who he works for?"

"Why do I know that name?" Carver said.

"I'm going to hate it, aren't I?" I asked.

"Yep," Jack said. "William Kirby works for the state department."

"Well, that's a real bummer," Carver said, shoving a bite of eggs into his mouth.

"Why? What does that mean?" I asked. "Kirby wasn't in Ukraine on a peace mission. He was there with Sowers buying underage girls."

"You know that, and I know that, and Kirby

knows that," Jack said. "But our case and our jurisdiction is to investigate the murder of David Sowers. We can't touch Kirby on the trafficking and he knows that. You should have seen the smug look on his face as Cole and I talked to him this morning. He, of course, knew about Sowers' drug problem. They all did, and were very concerned. He even tried to get him into rehab on multiple occasions."

"Uh-huh," I said. "And I've got oceanfront property in Nebraska I can sell you too. What about his trips to Ukraine?"

"Just business trips for the state department," Jack said. "All classified and they don't have anything to do with Sowers' murder. And since Kirby was sitting at the table with Sowers when he was shot he's not the killer. None of them pulled the trigger, so we had to cut them all loose."

"So despite the drugs and the trafficking, the only thing we can really focus on is the murder?" I asked.

"If we uncover more on the drugs or his supplier we can look deeper, but right now we only have Sowers' personal stash. As far as the trafficking, the man responsible is dead and Kirby is untouchable. So for right now, yes, we focus on the murder."

"That sucks," I said, dropping my bacon to my plate.

"You going to eat that?" Carver asked, reaching for the bacon. I slapped at his hand and said, "Yes. Because my cholesterol is just fine."

"Mean," Carver said, shaking his head.

Jack pushed his empty plate away and focused on his coffee. "I will say the others we interviewed were a lot more nervous than Kirby when we brought up the drugs and started talking about Sowers' penchant for underage girls. I think if we keep leaning on them they might come up with a few good suspects for who the shooter could be.

"Jasmine Taylor especially looked a little green around the gills. I mentioned the fact that a man like Sowers never did his own dirty work. He wasn't out on the street buying drugs. He wasn't the one who leased apartments or made sure his wife never intermingled with his lovers. And then I mentioned Kirby. There was something there. She was scared. But she told me to talk to Colby Chan. Apparently Chan is Sowers' admin. He was also at the dinner table when Sowers was killed. She said Chan took care of all of Sowers' needs."

"Convenient," I said.

"And nice of her to throw him under the bus like that," Carver said.

"My thoughts too."

"So our victim is basically the scum of the earth, who surrounds himself with more scum of the earth. And his depravity is common knowledge, and he doesn't bother to hide what he is to those who know him. Having people in higher up positions, like Kirby, made Sowers feel safe. He was cocky."

"And a liability," Jack said, reading my train of thought.

"A guy at the state department could easily get papers—passports, IDs, credit cards. Right?" I asked.

"Yes," Jack said. "Trafficking is a crime of power and money. It's not a poor man's sport. Both money and power corrupt, and for those who are already corrupt at heart it turns corruption to evil. We're living in a time of evil. You cut the head off one and ten more come back in its place. Look what's happening with Carver."

"It's a moral compass," Carver said, for once his tone serious. "I know whoever is doing this to me is high up on the food chain and has more power than I do. But there are other people at the top of the food chain of other agencies willing to step in and cut them down. Do I believe it's because of their sense of justice and right and wrong? No, I don't. I believe they do it because it's a means to an end. It helps their own agenda. And I have to live with that because my family and their safety is my first priority. So I'll go through the motions and keep cutting the head off one snake at a time. Just like what you're doing by catching a murderer. He's a snake. Is he as big of a snake as Sowers and Kirby?" Carver shrugged. "Who's to say? Probably not. But you have to start somewhere."

Jack blew out a breath. I'd seen the discouragement in him over the last months. He'd been serving this country and the people for a long time. But such as the way of the world, things don't ever really get better, because corruption spreads like yeast through a loaf of bread. I could tell with every case we took on that Jack was burning out more and more. As a wife, I wanted to fix the pain I saw in him. I wanted to protect him at all costs. The problem was I had no idea how to do so.

"All we can do is keep being a light to those who are hopeless," Carver said. "And on that note I will send you a bill for my hourly therapy rate. I've got to have a fallback now that I'm unemployed."

"Were you ever really employed?" I asked,

curiously. "It always kind of felt like you were your own entity, and then the FBI just recently noticed you were going rogue."

"Eh," Carver said, shrugging. "The truth is I do what I want to do. I have access to everyone's psych and IQ tests. Believe me, some of those people should barely hold a pencil, much less a gun."

"Good to know," Jack said. "As long as you're unemployed, maybe you could tell us something we don't know about our victim. Even with the warrant it'll take some time to get into his financials and sort everything out."

"I don't mean to throw water on a return to the good old days," I said. "But isn't Carver in danger of being caught here? We can't just put him to work like nothing else is going on his life."

"I'm as safe here under their noses as anywhere," Carver said. "Besides, I led them on a false trail showing I've been using my credit cards all the way down the coast toward Florida." He looked at his watch. "And right about now, the FBI is waiting for me to show up at the Miami airport. Apparently I have plans to fly out today and head to Aruba."

"I hear it's nice this time of year," I said.

Carver sighed. "I've heard that too. I don't

have plans to stay here long, but I can do a couple of quick searches for you and send them to you. I'll take off after you guys leave to go talk to the widow. Don't worry about the yahoos sticking around here in Bloody Mary. Their orders are to keep an eye on you, not interrogate you about my whereabouts. One of them is a rookie and he forwarded his orders to his personal email. I could've found out what they were planning without the stupidity involved, but stupidity always helps a little."

"Just don't get cocky," Jack said. "They know how you operate and that nothing electronic is sacred."

"Duly noted," Carver said. "I'll be careful. I promise. And as long as you guys don't act like you're in any way interested in what's happened to me or they don't overhear you talking about me, they should leave you alone. If you pop up on their radar for anything deeper I'll try to let you know ahead of time."

He was inputting information into Magnolia while he was talking, and then he said, "I pulled all of your victim's data from the autopsy report Jaye filed. Hope you don't mind. Your officers haven't filed the police report yet."

Jack smiled. "They've been a little busy. I

don't even know why we use passwords with you around."

"Me either," Carver said. "Martinez's password is his birthday and Cole's changes pretty frequently to the name of whatever woman he's dating at the time. Probably helps him remember her name."

Jack blew out a patient sigh. "Anything on Sowers?"

"Got all the basics—physical description, weight, height—no criminal record. All bills currently up to date. Looks like he's got a few rental properties."

"Is one of them the apartment downtown?" Jack asked.

"Nothing downtown," Carver said, shaking his head. "He owns the building where his law office is in King George. All of the other suites are rented out and bring in a healthy income. He's got a duplex unit also in King George near the college, and a smattering of houses all over the county. He owns a condo on Dupont Circle in DC."

"That doesn't come cheap," I said.

"He's got an office in DC too," Carver said. "Looks like he travels back and forth to DC quite a bit. What's the address of the apartment downtown?"

Jack gave it to him and Carver did a reverse search.

"Good investment property," Carver said. "I see you guys own a couple of units. Diversifying your portfolio is smart. Always good to have something to fall back on if this whole law enforcement thing doesn't work out."

"Yeah, we're dipping a toe in," Jack said, laughter in his eyes.

I knew Jack's family was wealthy. And I knew that we had money. But I had no idea the extent of how far that reached. I wasn't sure I wanted to know.

"Looks like the corner apartment is owned by a company called Clandestine," Carver continued. "Let's do a look and see what that is." He was silent for several minutes. "Ahh, this is more interesting by the minute. And it's going to take a little time. Looks like Clandestine is owned by a company called Q.T., and Q.T. is owned by a company called Insidious."

"Clever word play," I said, rolling my eyes. "As if I didn't already dislike this guy enough."

"No names associated with any of them," Carver said. "Well done, well done." He was talking to himself now, and I could see the gleam of excitement in his eyes. It was rare that Carver was challenged by anything.

"Sounds like state department interference to me," Jack said. "William Kirby is the fly in the ointment. But we've got to move past it. What about finances?"

"I can dig deeper, especially now that I've got the names of these shell corporations, but on the surface everything seems to be aboveboard. Sowers' mother served on Bill Clinton's cabinet for four years. Both parents were high-profile attorneys and were in and out of politics until their deaths. Sowers inherited well. Graduated from Harvard Law. Married the daughter of a governor. On paper, they were being groomed for politics and to be the next golden couple."

"What happened?" Jack asked.

"Just a second," Carver said. "Magnolia, search for newspaper articles and media reports surrounding a car crash David Sowers and his first wife were involved in. The year is 1987."

"Sure thing, sugar," Magnolia said. "I was wondering when you were going to include me."

"You could have jumped in at any time," Carver said, dismissively.

I just closed my eyes and shook my head.

"What?" Carver asked, looking at me.

"It's like you don't know anything about women," I said. "I'm constantly fascinated considering you have a wife and four daughters."

"All we want is love and attention," Magnolia said. "You'll get a chance to make it up to me."

"Glory be," Carver mouthed silently.

"There are several hits from major news sources matching those dates and names," Magnolia said. "Fatality car crash involving Sowers and his wife on Christmas Eve. Sowers drove into oncoming traffic and hit a minivan, killing a family of four instantly. There was an investigation to determine if alcohol was involved, but all major news sources cited that toxicology came back clear."

"Why do I feel like there's a but coming on," Carver said.

"There are several smaller, local papers that say Sowers and his wife were coming home from a party and they had both been drinking heavily. The sources come from witnesses at the party. They later all had to retract the story."

Carver picked up the story, scanning the documents coming up on the screen quickly. "It looks like Sowers ran for a state rep spot in Virginia in the next election cycle, but his opponent cast enough suspicion about the accident that Sowers lost by a landslide. He never ran for another election, choosing to align himself politically in other ways. But by looking at his tax returns and investments, whatever he was doing panned out well for him. The first wife died of cancer about fifteen years ago."

"Anything we need to know about the current wife?"

"Nia Sowers," Carver said. "She looks clean. Grew up wealthy. Parents were killed in a car crash when she was fifteen. She graduated from an exclusive boarding school in London and then married Sowers a week after graduation and about two weeks after the first wife died."

"Gross," I said.

"He does have a type," Jack said. "Guys like him are the reason it scares me to death to think about bringing a daughter into this world."

"That's why I try not to think about it too much," I said. "Otherwise we'd never be on the same page about having children."

"I feel like I'm missing something important," Carver said. "Am I about to be an uncle? You did eat that breakfast unusually fast. You should probably lay off the caffeine though."

I closed my eyes. "I'm not pregnant. We're just talking about it. Why does everyone keep asking me that?"

"Maybe because you keep talking about it," Carver said. "Just do it."

"Thank you, Carver," Jack said dryly. "We'll get right on it. Speaking of getting right on it, they should be ready to serve the warrant on the wife. I want to question her while they're still there."

"Don't worry about me," Carver said. "I'll see myself out."

CHAPTER NINE

"WHAT'S ON YOUR MIND?" JACK ASKED, TAKING the exit toward King George proper.

"So many things," I said carefully.

I remembered what Carver had said about not talking outside the walls of our house about anything he'd shared with us. It also hadn't gone past my notice that a dark sedan had been following at least two cars behind us ever since we left Bloody Mary.

"Babies?" Jack asked, and I could hear the smile in his voice.

"No," I said. "Maybe a little. But I'm curious as to what kind of woman could be married to a man like David Sowers. She'd know something— whether about his drug habit or the other women—wives always know."

"She was barely eighteen when they married," Jack said. "She might not have had a choice."

Jack sped up a little, and then he swerved over two lanes and took an exit at the last minute. We watched the dark sedan pass by, unable to get over in time to follow.

"Whoops," Jack said.

"Are you really that worried about bringing children into the world?" I asked. "Maybe we shouldn't. What if we're neurotic? I mean, we know what people are capable of. Most people have no idea of the evil that lives around them or the kind of danger their children are in."

"No," Jack said. "I don't think we shouldn't do it because we know the reality of what could happen. I think it'll make us really good parents."

We were silent for the rest of the drive to the Sowers' house.

"Figures," I said, when we pulled up in front of a white elephant of a house. It was sleek and modern, and I wasn't a hundred percent sure where the door was, but that might have been the point. I couldn't imagine Sowers wanted his neighbors popping by. "I'm not sure I've ever seen a more unwelcoming house."

"Maybe the house from *The Texas Chainsaw Massacre*," Jack said flippantly.

"Or Lizzie Borden's," I said. "Though I kind of always thought that house was cute."

"Except for the dismembered bodies in the windows."

"I'm sure they've cleaned it since then," I said, rolling my eyes. "Those crime scene teams work miracles."

I noticed the squad cars parked along the street, and the front door was open as a deputy carried a box out the front door.

"Cole and Martinez are going to be mad they're missing this," Jack said. "They love serving warrants."

"Odd," I said. "Considering that's typically when people try to shoot at you."

"Depends on the kind of warrant," Jack said, grinning. "But they like to serve those too."

"I'm not sure how healthy it is to have a bunch of lunatics with a death wish running around in uniform," I said. "And you know how men are. The more of them that get together the worse the decisions they make."

"I've always said it takes a special kind of crazy to be a cop," Jack said.

"And I married it," I said, patting him lightly on the butt where no one else could see.

Jack snickered and then his face went stoic as we approached the open door. He knocked on the doorframe and then stepped inside as a woman in black leggings and a soft sweater the color of blueberries came down the stairs to meet us.

I'd been expecting a woman in her early thirties, but somehow Nia Sowers seemed even younger. She looked like she'd just had the rug swept out from under her. Her honey-blond hair was swept up into a loose ponytail, and there were dark circles under her eyes. She was a tall woman with sharp features that probably photographed beautifully.

"Mrs. Sowers?" Jack asked.

When she stared at Jack with emptiness I was reminded of Kateryna—they both carried the same look of defeat and hopelessness.

"Call me Nia," she said. "Please come in."

I detected the slightest accent, but it didn't sound British.

"We know this is a difficult time for you," Jack said. "And we appreciate any help you can give us in finding out who did this to your husband."

"I need a drink," she said, leading us into a living room that had an eerie similarity to the apartment where Kateryna lived. She stood behind a bar that was almost as well stocked as the Purple Pig had been. "If you add orange juice to your vodka, Americans don't look at you quite so strange if you drink before noon. Would you like some?"

"No, thank you," I said. "I've already reached my limit for the day."

Her smile was quick, and she poured a healthy amount of vodka over ice and then a splash of orange juice to give it color. She rattled the ice in the glass before taking a sip. "That is funny. I did not realize cops had a sense of humor."

"I'm not a cop," I said. "I'm a coroner. Coroners definitely have a sense of humor."

"Good to know," she said.

"I can't place your accent," Jack said, taking a seat so he could see the entire room. Officers were moving all around, going through drawers and collecting files and electronics.

She frowned slightly and said, "My husband would be upset to know that my accent is still detectable by strangers. I've worked hard to rid myself of it over the years."

"I think it shows you're human," I said. "Strong emotion tends to take us back to what is familiar. You've had a lot of strong emotions in the last twenty-four hours."

She sighed and took the seat across from us, her back facing the stairs.

"I was born in South Africa and I lived there until I was ten," she said.

"And then what?" Jack asked.

She stared at Jack for several seconds without responding. "I've not spoken of my family in a very long time. It was best I forgot them altogether."

"Your file says your parents were killed in a car crash when you were fifteen," Jack said.

"David gave me my past," she said. "He told me it would be easier if I thought of them as dead."

"You could find them now," Jack said. "We could help you track them down."

Her expression was stoic, her gaze empty of all emotion. "They would not want me after the life I've lived. It is better to start over."

"When was the last time you saw them?" he asked.

"I suppose it doesn't matter if I speak of them now," she said. "There is no one here to care." She crossed her legs and rattled the ice in her glass once more. "We went on family holiday to St. Petersburg one summer and that was the last time I saw them. My parents. My two brothers. My father was in shipping. We took nice trips every year. One moment I was at the museum playing hide and go seek with my brothers, and I hid behind a suit of armor. And the next moment there is just darkness."

"When did you meet David Sowers?"

"I was fifteen," she said. "I thought he was my knight in shining armor." She shrugged. "Maybe he was. I know there are much worse fates than the life I've lived. I was living in a home with thirty other girls. It was hard not to be flattered that he chose me. But he was a troubled man."

"Troubled enough that someone wanted him dead," Jack said.

"It does not surprise me," she said. "I'm sure there are many who would have taken pleasure in it."

"The truth is going to come out about him," Jack said. "About what he did to you. And the others. There are other girls like you."

She nodded. "I know. I do not know them personally, but I have overheard conversations. They are just children. Like I was."

"He was a bad man," Jack said. "And you were a victim. None of this was your fault."

"I'm glad he's dead," she said, looking away. "That is a terrible thing to say. I have a good life. I have this house. Everything I need. And he leaves me alone. I am..."

"Too old?" Jack finished for her.

She nodded, looking relieved that he understood. "Yes. We have been married twelve years. He hasn't touched me in ten."

"You have no children?" Jack asked.

Grief etched the lines of her face. "No," she said. "He never wanted children. His career always came first, even with his first wife."

"I noticed during the autopsy that he had a prosthetic testicle," I said. "Do you know the cause?"

She closed her eyes and her cheeks flushed in embarrassment. "He was drunk," she said. "And he fell down the stairs and somehow the pen in his pocket..." she made a motion with her hand and we got the gist of what she was trying to say. I could almost feel Jack's wince.

"Did you know his first wife?" I asked.

"No," she said. "Only from photographs. He enrolled me in a finishing school in London after he chose me. He told me I needed to be able to speak to diplomats and other important people, and I had an aptitude for academia. I learned very quickly. I believe he saw me as an asset and that's why he chose me."

"No one ever asked questions about your age or your circumstances?" I asked her.

"No," she said. "I had forged papers while we were in London, and David was listed as my legal guardian. He called me his daughter. For some reason, that designation made what we were doing seem all the more exciting to him."

She shuddered lightly and looked down at her drink, realizing it was empty. She moved back to the bar for a refill.

"He spoke of his wife from time to time and his business partners. I knew he was a successful attorney. He would bring clients to the house in London and give me to them as a welcome gift. I was to always do what the client wanted." She shrugged, as if it were just a way of life. "I was beaten on many occasions. But once I was beaten so badly I wanted to die. David was angry with me because I fought back. I wasn't supposed to fight back. I clawed at the man's face and left marks. When he was finished he left and David came in with a knife. I was still bloody and lying on the floor. He held the tip of the knife at my eye and told me if I ever displeased him like that again then I'd only wish I was dead. I believed him."

"How old were you?" I asked.

"Maybe sixteen," she said. "It's hard to remember. He left after that and didn't come back to visit for a long time. I kept expecting my schooling to stop or to be taken away, but it didn't. So I knew that he would be back. I woke up dreading the day of his return.

"And then one day he showed up and said his wife died and that I was to take her place," she said. "My schooling was finished. He gave me new papers with a new date of birth and age. The papers already had me as his wife so we could travel freely together. Even my citizenship had been changed to American."

"How old were you really?" Jack asked.

She smiled and drained the glass. "It was my seventeenth birthday."

"Do you know a William Kirby?" Jack asked.

"The name is not familiar," she said, shaking her head. "Is he the man who killed David?"

"No," Jack asked. "Had your husband gotten any threats? Did anything come here to the house that might have been suspicious?"

"Not that I know of," she said. "I always put his mail and packages on the desk in his office. I'm not to touch anything in there or open his mail."

"What about drugs?" I asked.

She hesitated and looked down, as if she were deciding how to answer. "Yes, I believe he was taking something. I found a package taped to the back of the toilet upstairs. There were many drugs in the house I'd lived in before David, so I recognized what it was. I didn't say anything to him about it, but sometimes he would have terrible fits of rage. I always stayed out of the way or left the house. It was never good to be too close to him during those times."

"How about money?" Jack asked. "Did he ever seem worried about money? Or owe money to anyone?"

"I know nothing about those things," she said. "I'm given an allowance every week, but that is all I know about our money."

Jack nodded and stood up, and I followed suit. "We're sorry for the inconvenience of having to go through your home."

"I understand," she said. "I guess I am trying to get used to the fact that he will not walk through the doors again. I'm not sure what to do next."

"Take all the time you need," Jack said. "You might discover you have dreams of your own."

She laughed softly as if the thought were unimaginable and we let ourselves out.

CHAPTER TEN

"Breakfast seems like years ago," I said once we left the Sowers' neighborhood.

"I'm assuming that means you're ready for lunch?" Jack asked. "That chicken salad place is up here. We can drive through."

"I want the kind with the little grapes in it," I said. "Nia Sowers was lying about not knowing Kirby."

"Yeah, I picked up on that," Jack said, getting in the drive-thru line. "The question is why."

"Most obvious reason would be that she's scared of him," I said. "If he's the one who has control over her legal status or papers maybe she's afraid what he'll do to her, especially now that Sowers is dead." I paused to look at the long line. "Good grief. Who knew chicken salad was so popular."

"It's the new boba tea," Jack said. "All the fads fade at some point."

"I just don't understand why people want chewy balls in their tea," I said. "I don't drink things just so I can chew. It makes no sense."

Jack grinned and tapped his fingers on the wheel. I amused him.

The phone rang and Jack hit a button on the steering wheel to answer. "What's up, Cole?"

"Thought you'd want to know we've got a visual of Bobby Pickering," Cole said. "We got a hit back after we put his picture on the news as a person of interest. He's eating lunch bold as you please at Heart Attack Burgers in King George."

"We're two minutes away," Jack said, pulling out of the line and heading back on the highway. "What's your feel? You think he's oblivious?"

"No, I think he's meeting someone," Cole said. "He keeps glancing at the door and he hasn't ordered yet. Seems impatient. I was waiting to see if anyone else showed up before we moved on him."

"Your call," Jack said. "What's your twenty?"

"I'm across the street at the coffee shop," Cole said. "He's in clear view. Martinez is in the alley behind the restaurant and I've got plainclothes guys on each end of the street."

"I'm circling behind the coffee shop," Jack said. "I don't want him to see my unit."

Jack parked by a dumpster, and we got out of the Tahoe quickly, using the back entrance of the coffee shop closest to the bathrooms.

"Good timing," Cole said as we came up to the bistro table he was occupying in the corner.

Cole had been right. Bobby Pickering was in his direct line of sight, but the angle made it so Pickering couldn't see us unless he turned his head a little more.

"Any sign of who he's meeting?" Jack asked.

"Not yet," Cole said.

"Wait a sec," Jack said, nodding toward the opposite corner. "That guy look familiar?"

Cole shook his head, but then I remembered Cole had already left for the night when we interviewed the valets.

"Oh," I said. "That's the kid from last night. Darnell?"

"Bingo," Jack said. "What do you want to bet that's who Pickering is waiting for?"

Cole brought a walkie-talkie to his mouth and said, "Plank, you've got a potential suspect coming from behind you. Black jacket and gray beanie. Hands in his pockets."

There was silence for a bit and then Plank said, "Got him."

I saw a teenager who'd been propping up a corner of the building looking at his cell phone start following Darnell and my mouth dropped open.

"Is that Plank?" I asked in surprise.

"The one and only," Cole said, grinning.

Plank was a rookie officer who was slowly getting the shine rubbed off of him, but he still looked like a fresh-faced kid playing dress-up in his father's uniform. But today he looked even younger wearing a hoodie and baggy jeans and an old baseball cap. His cheeks were flushed red from the cold and his sneakers looked nice but well used. As he walked closer, I could tell he had AirPods in his ears and he was moving to an unheard beat as he made his way down the sidewalk.

Darnell opened the door of the restaurant and stepped inside and Plank kept going, not giving up his cover.

"Wow," I said. "I'm not sure I would've recognized him if he'd come in here."

"The kid's good," Cole said. "Just young. If we can get Wachowski to make a man out of him one day he's going to be a heck of a cop."

Jack snorted out a laugh. Plank and

Wachowski had recently gone from the dating each other phase to living together. Wachowski was a seasoned cop and a good eight years older than Plank, and Plank's parents weren't thrilled with the arrangement, but no one had died yet, so we all considered that a win.

Cole lifted the walkie-talkie again and said, "Let's move. Nice and slow. I don't feel like running today."

Cole got up from the table and we waited until Plank had turned around and entered the restaurant. His hand was in the pocket of his hoodie where I assumed his weapon was. Another officer I recognized as Holmes came in shortly after Plank, and then we followed Cole out of the coffee shop and across the street. Darnell's back was to us, so he didn't see us enter. But it was obvious Pickering was familiar with cops, because as soon as he saw Cole and Jack enter the restaurant he moved to get up from the table.

Fortunately, Plank and Holmes were standing right there and Plank put his hand on Pickering's shoulder, pushing him back down into his seat.

"Fancy seeing you here, Darnell," Jack said as he came up to the table.

Darnell had a deer in the headlights look and

he swallowed several times, looking back and forth between Jack and Pickering.

"Bobby Pickering," Cole said. "We've been looking for you. Need to ask you some questions about what happened at the Purple Pig last night. The best thing you can do is come with us peacefully. We'll walk right out of here and take a trip to the station." Then Cole looked at Darnell. "Looks like we need to ask you some questions too."

Plank still had his hand on Pickering's shoulder and moved it to his arm to help Pickering out of the booth.

There was a loud explosion and the next thing I knew I was covered in blood and brain matter. I saw Pickering crumple to the ground. His head was all but gone, but then I saw Plank go down with him.

There was no time to duck or take cover. No time to react. One moment we'd been standing there and the next there was carnage. I'd been through a lot in my life. I'd had life-or-death experiences, more than I'd have preferred. I'd felt the life drain from me slowly and I'd had my life flash before my eyes with the violence created by evil. But never had I been so close to the fragility of the human body, and so close to the bullet that caused the destruction.

For a moment I was frozen. I'd never been frozen before, at least not when other lives were in danger. But I was paralyzed, trying with every gasp of breath to get my mind to wrap around what I was looking at. I couldn't put a thought together. The only thing there was fear.

"Down," I heard someone yell, but all sound was distorted, as if I were underwater and I could only hear my own screaming in my head.

"Jaye," Jack said, taking me by both arms and looking into my eyes. "Jaye," he said again. "Focus on me and breathe. You're okay."

The more I focused on his voice, the clearer it became, and the sound whooshed back to my ears as if someone had suddenly turned up the volume on the radio. Jack was covered in blood and I had a moment of panic that it was his.

"It's not mine," he said, reading my thoughts. "I'm fine. But Plank needs some help. Sit down and breathe."

I almost did as he told me, but something kicked in from deep inside and I shook my head, willing myself back to reality.

"I'm okay," I said, my voice coming out in a croak. "I'm okay."

I knelt down next to Plank, trying to assess the damage and remember my training. "Did anyone call 911?" I asked.

"On the way," Martinez said, standing behind me. "Sheriff, we've got officers en route. There's only one place that shot could've come from. What do you want to do?"

I could hear the sirens as police cars swarmed the area and the accompanying yells as people were ordered back so they could block off the streets.

"Take a team and go," Jack said. "Be careful. He's elevated. He'll see you coming if he hasn't already moved out."

I was trying to assess Plank, but it was almost impossible to determine the source of his wound. He'd been standing closest to Pickering and he was covered in blood, bone, and tissue. It made sense that the bullet that had done that much damage to Pickering's head would've found another target. And Plank had been that target.

I found the entry wound just under his collarbone, and I felt behind him to see if there was an exit wound. There wasn't, which was good news for Plank. Someone shoved a towel into my hand and I applied pressure, ignoring the fact that my own hand was shaking.

"You with me, Plank?" I asked, grabbing his wrist with one hand and searching for his pulse. It was fast, but it was strong.

His lips moved as if he were trying to speak,

but he pressed them together tightly through the pain.

"You're going to be okay," I said. "But that collarbone is probably hurting pretty bad."

"Bullet hurts too," he said between gritted teeth.

"Thattaboy," I said. "Deep breaths. Slow exhale. EMTs are on the way. Just think of how good Wachowski is going to treat you after this. Waiting on you hand and foot. Sponge baths."

"She's going to be so mad," Plank whispered. "I'd almost rather die."

I heard the EMTs coming in behind me and the familiar sound of the gurney as it rolled across the floor. I felt hands take over the pressure and I moved out of the way so I was sitting against the booth on the floor. I didn't trust my legs to stand back up. My arms rested limply on my knees and I hung my head taking in deep breaths and trying not to think what clung to my skin and hair.

I wasn't sure how long I sat there, but I'd appreciated that everyone had left me alone. I knew Jack had a job to do, and I also knew he was worried about me. But I couldn't ask him to stop his responsibilities just to make sure I didn't fall apart.

"Dr. Graves," someone said. I didn't recognize

the voice, and I had trouble lifting my head to see who it was.

It was one of the crime scene techs. I'd seen her at the Purple Pig, but I didn't know her by name.

"I'm Officer Daniels," she said. She had a kind, round face and dark eyes. Her dark hair was in tight braids and brushed the tops of her shoulders. "We need to collect the evidence from you and get you cleaned up."

"Right," I said, letting her help me to my feet.

"We've got a curtained area set up over here," she said. "You'll need to remove your clothing so we can bag it, and then we'll get the particulates from your hair."

I closed my eyes and tried not to visualize what I must look like, but then I saw Jack and Cole behind one of the curtained areas, their chests bare and their jaws clenched tight as a couple of techs removed pieces of flesh and bone from their hair.

Holmes and Darnell were inside another curtained area receiving the same treatment, though it didn't look as if they'd had as much spatter as the rest of us. They'd both been standing on the other side of the table so it made sense. I also noticed Darnell was handcuffed to one of the metal poles.

"You get your own tent," Officer Daniels said.

"Lucky me," I said, looking at what appeared to be four yellow sheets that were hung with a prayer on a shower curtain rod.

She chuckled and helped me disrobe carefully, so I didn't displace any evidence. "Some job, huh?" she asked. "You're gonna be okay. Just a little rattled right now. Perfectly understandable. Got some bullet fragments here."

She just went about her business as if this were the most normal thing in the world, carrying on a soothing stream of chatter. I wasn't sure what caused it. Maybe I just needed the mothering touch of another women. But I felt the tears drip onto my cheeks and there wasn't anything I could do to stop them.

"There, there," she said. "Almost done. Sometimes it's just too much and we've got to let our minds process. You've got to take care of you first or you're no good to anyone. You take my advice, cause we're gonna be here awhile picking up body parts. You go home and take a good shower, get something hot to eat and take a nap. You'll feel right as rain if you do."

"How we doing, Daniels?" Jack asked as he and Cole left their tent.

They were both wearing what looked like

paper scrubs, and dried blood was still streaked on their faces.

"Getting closer, sheriff," Daniels said. "My girl is going to be good as new before too long."

I finally found the courage to meet Jack's gaze and I saw the worry there. I still hadn't managed to stop the tears.

"Sometimes you've just got to put a pause on an investigation and take a shower," Jack said.

"Amen, sheriff," Daniels said. "Amen."

My voice had never really recovered completely after I'd been strangled a couple of years ago, and I'd developed a raspy Lauren Bacall-type voice Jack told me was sexy. There were moments when I felt my vocal cords freeze and I couldn't manage to make the sounds my brain was communicating, so when I opened my mouth to speak the sound that came out wasn't what I was looking for.

But eventually the words came. "Did Martinez catch him?" I asked.

Jack shook his head. "The guy was gone by the time they got up to the roof across the street. He was literally staked out right above where we were talking with Cole in the coffee shop. He didn't leave his casing behind this time, and we have a potential witness who said a Caucasian or possibly Hispanic male bumped into her on the sidewalk and got into a small white four-door sedan."

"I was expecting a manlier car," I said.

"White four-door sedans are the most common in America," Jack said. "Perfect way to blend in. There's probably half a dozen parked at the meters along this stretch of road. She wasn't able to give us any identifying markers. He was wearing a black coat, gloves, and a watch cap pulled low. He also had on sunglasses and a scarf. Hardly any of his face was showing."

"There we go," Daniels said, closing up the last evidence bag. She took a wet wipe and let me wipe my face and mouth, and then she handed me a pair of paper scrubs like Jack was wearing.

"There's nothing else we can do here now," Jack said. "Time for a shower and lunch. In that order."

"I'm not going to argue with that plan," I said.

"Thattagirl, Doc," Daniels said. "See you next time."

I stopped and looked at her in the eyes so she'd see my sincerity. "Thank you," I told her. "Truly. You were a gift."

"There's all kinds of ways to protect and serve," she said, patting my hand.

CHAPTER ELEVEN

THE HOUSE WAS QUIET WHEN WE ARRIVED HOME, and there was no sign of Carver. On the kitchen table was a file folder filled with several sheets of paper. I couldn't even think about the case right now.

"I'm going to shower in the bathroom next to the laundry room," I said. "I'm afraid what residue I'll track upstairs."

Jack grunted and I took off the paper scrubs on the way to the bathroom, shoving them in the big trash can inside the laundry room. My hands and around my nails were stained pink, and I didn't bother to look at my face in the mirror.

I turned the water on blistering hot and stepped into the shower, watching the water turn to red as it spiraled down the drain. I didn't fight the tears, but I let them fall freely as I scrubbed every inch of skin until it stung. I washed my hair three times, hoping that was enough, and then I stepped out of the shower and dried off, glad the mirror was too fogged to see my reflection.

I hadn't thought ahead about fresh clothes, but Jack had. He always thought of the details and there was a soft gray sweat suit and underwear sitting on the vanity.

I put on the clothes and then wrapped my wet head in a towel, and then padded out to the kitchen where Jack was making sandwiches. He was wearing a similar sweat suit and his feet were bare. It wasn't often Jack kept quiet, but he'd been a man of few words since the incident.

I took a seat at the bar across from him and watched him assemble BLTs with efficient movements.

"So," I said. "Interesting day."

Jack took the chef's knife from the block and cut both of our sandwiches down the middle. I flinched at the sound of the force as the knife hit the wood cutting block, and then raised my brows as he arranged the sandwiches on plates in silence and then put one in front of me.

Then he leaned both hands on the countertop and dropped his head. "I don't know how long I can keep doing this," he said.

"Being a cop?" I asked, surprised.

"No," he said. "Watching you in the line of fire. It's always been different when it was just me. You don't think about those things going into a situation, otherwise you'd never put on the badge. But it's another thing entirely to watch it happen to your wife. How many times over the last years has your life been in danger? How many times has it been too close of a call? You were inches away from that bullet. If his trajectory had even been the slightest bit off it would've been your head they'd have been picking off of me."

He shook his head and pushed back from the counter, pacing back and forth like a caged tiger.

"I can tell you right now I'm not strong enough for that," he said. "Watching you escape death time and time again has taken years off my life. And it's made me realize that I don't think I can be here on this earth without you. I literally feel torn in two. I don't know what to do anymore. I know that you're who you are and you do what you do. I'd never expect you to be anything different. But I can't keep watching your life hang in the balance."

Jack rarely showed this level of emotion. He was always steady in a crisis, always the one who held his emotions in check so he could think rationally. But the man pacing before me looked anything but rational, and it certainly didn't seem like his emotions were in check.

I thought about all the things I could say to deescalate the situation. I could've reassured him that I was alive and well. I could've reminded him that there were dangers involved in the kind of work we'd chosen. But Jack deserved better than piecrust promises that were easily made and easily broken.

"I'm going to share an important piece of advice with you," I said, moving around the bar and walking straight into him, leaving him no choice but to wrap his arms around me.

"What's that?" he asked soberly.

"It comes from my new friend Officer Daniels," I said. "Sometimes the only thing you need in life to feel better is something to eat and a nap. So I propose we take these sandwiches that you took your anger out on upstairs and then we check out for a couple of hours. Let's see how we feel then."

"Hmm," Jack said, resting his forehead against mine. "Sound advice." I felt his body relax as he exhaled. "I've seen a lot of things in my career. And I almost lost you once. But I have to say I've never been as scared as I was today. I don't want to ever feel that way again."

He leaned back and squeezed my hands before letting me go. "But you're right," he said. "Officer Daniels always gives good advice. We don't have to solve the problem right now. Let's get some rest."

"I'm going to send Officer Daniels a fruit basket," I said two hours later. "And you should give her a raise. She's a wise woman."

I felt something hard beneath my hip and shifted, grabbing the empty plate that had once held my sandwich. Apparently, I'd eaten and immediately fallen asleep, because I didn't remember anything happening in between my last bite and my eyes closing.

"I've tried to promote her twice, but she keeps rejecting me," Jack said. "She's the best crime scene tech I have, but she doesn't want to be stuck in an office supervising. She wants to be in the field. Can't say I blame her."

I looked over at Jack. The sun was beginning to set behind the trees outside our window and his face was cast in a soft glow. He was still in his sweats and his fingers were entwined loosely over his stomach. Some of the tension was gone from his face, but I could tell he was in deep thought.

"We need to process information," I said. "My brain is scrambled. We've had two professional hits in less than twenty-four hours. And we've inadvertently uncovered a local trafficking network. There's also the potential of mob ties and military involvement."

Jack let out a deep sigh. "Yeah," he said. "One big mess. Let's just leave everything behind. We won't even pack a suitcase. We'll just get on a plane and go wherever it takes us, and we can start a new life. Maybe Kirby can give us new identities if we promise to leave him alone."

I snorted out a laugh and rolled out of bed.

"I feel like pizza," I said.

"You just had a sandwich."

"That was two hours ago. That counts as a snack. We need to feed our minds."

Jack got out of bed and went to stand by the windows, looking out at the view. Our house was built almost on the side of the cliff, so it looked like it was part of the scenery, and unseen below was the Potomac rushing against the rocks.

"We've got to talk about our future soon," Jack said. "Seriously. I want you to start thinking about where you see us in a year or five years. What do things look like?"

I opened my mouth to speak, but Jack stopped me.

"Not now," he said. "Case first. Just think on it, okay? And I promise to do the same."

I nodded and then we padded downstairs to the first floor. "It's crazy how quiet it is with Doug gone," I said. "He hasn't been here long, but I've gotten used to him."

"It's weird to me that we actually have food in the refrigerator," Jack said. "He's actually driving back tonight. He said his mom had a date and he didn't want to cramp her style. And it'll be nice for him to pick up the trail where Carver left off."

I'd almost been afraid to talk about Carver for fear of the feds breaking down the door. "How do you think he got out of here?"

"I don't know," Jack said, "But it's probably no coincidence that Doug was less than an hour away when he texted me. I have a feeling Carver's close ties are with the CIA. I'm not sure Carver has ever exclusively belonged to one agency. Carver is too valuable an asset to world organizations for the FBI to go making a mess of things. Wherever and whoever is the cause of corruption is going to regret it. Never underestimate Carver. He may look like a pencil pusher in a wheelchair, but I would still pick Carver to have my back in any situation." Then he winked at me. "If you weren't available, of course."

"Of course," I said. "I'll order the pizza."

"Order enough for everyone. And Doug. I'm going to call the guys and we'll set up the board here. I don't want to have to explain outside these walls where we got some of our information."

I was on the phone with the local pizza place when I heard the key in the lock and the front door open.

"I'm home!" Doug called out. "And I'm starving."

"Jaye's ordering food," Jack said. "And the guys will be here in a few minutes. Do you have Mackenzie?"

"Never leave home without her," Doug said as he came into the kitchen and dumped a duffle bag and his laptop case on the bar.

Doug was brilliant. Almost as brilliant as Carver, but he still had room to grow in both skill and common sense. When we'd first met Doug he'd been on house arrest for hacking the Pentagon. It had been Carver who'd caught him. Fortunately, Carver had put the fear of God in his nephew and he was on the side of law and order now.

I hung up the phone and said, "I'm sure Mackenzie is grateful to never be left out."

"Last time I left her alone she threw a fit and didn't talk to me for a week," Doug said, and then he whispered, "You know how nosy she is."

"She can hear you while she's closed?" I asked, realizing I was whispering as well.

"Oh, yeah," Doug said enthusiastically. "AI is progressing by leaps and bounds. There's no need for a Wi-Fi connection. In fact, AI has made it obsolete."

The doorbell rang and I heard male voices in the lobby talking to Jack. It had to be Cole and Martinez. And then I heard a lone female voice. Lily had come along too.

"Don't get me wrong," I told Doug, and then I whispered in his ear, "but your computer creeps me out."

Doug winced. "She really hates to be called a computer. She's got feelings."

"I'm just saying, there are movies made about this. And it never ends well for the humans."

He picked up the computer bag and followed me into the hallway, a goofy grin etched on his face.

"Hey, the kid is back," Cole said. "I thought you took off for the weekend."

"Yeah, that didn't go as planned," Doug said. "My mom is dating this guy. Their love is kind of gross. Besides, I had, uh, some stuff to do around here."

Doug glanced at Jack and then looked away quickly. Doug was going to have to work on his poker face if he planned to stay in the subterfuge game.

"Fun that you guys are being watched by the feds," Cole said, waggling his eyebrows. "They're not even bothering to hide. Or maybe they are and they're just bad at it. This bald guy in the driver's seat looks kind of dumb."

"They've got taxpayer money to waste," Jack said.

"You think you're bugged?" Martinez asked.

"I think they probably tried," Jack said. "But Carver did our security system. They're probably trying to figure out what's wrong with their equipment."

Lily wove her way through the large male bodies blocking the way and shed her coat and scarf. "I'm so sick of this weather. It's the winter that will never end."

"Technically it is still winter," Martinez reminded her."

"Shut up," she said good-naturedly. "It just seems like it's been longer than normal. I need sunshine and a bikini."

"I'm a big supporter of both of those things," Cole said.

"Did you get called into the crime scene?" I asked Lily as we made our way to Jack's office.

"Yep," she said. "They said you were incapacitated so I bagged the remains and escorted it back to the lab. Sheldon actually threw up. Then he told me that a study was done and most people couldn't tell the difference between parmesan cheese and vomit. So I probably won't ever enjoy Italian food again."

"Good to know," I said. "We ordered pizza tonight."

She shrugged and said, "Eh, I'll suffer through it. Anyway, the victim is ready for you to autopsy and the tissue evidence is in the fridge. He sure was a mess."

"Understatement of the year," I said.

Jack's office was one of my favorite rooms in the house. It was as big as the living room and was complete with a fireplace and floor-to-ceiling windows that had automated privacy screens when we were working on sensitive information. The furniture in front of the fireplace was cozy and masculine and a great place to curl up with a book. And the other half of the room was all business with a large conference table and Jack's desk.

But my favorite part of the room was the computer wall. The two corner walls connected and looked like a floor-to-ceiling whiteboard, but it was really a computer. Jack could run everything on it from his laptop or iPad, and it could run multiple functions at a time. Carver had designed it for us. But if it started talking back to me like Magnolia or Mackenzie we were going to have problems.

Doug sat in one of the black leather chairs at the conference table and set up Mackenzie, while Jack pulled up the information that had already been put into the police database.

Jack started by putting up the information on our two victims. David Sowers' face went up on-screen—first his DMV photo followed by the crime scene photo. He looked like a man who always got what he wanted. Even his driver's license picture oozed with intimidation and malice.

"I prefer the death picture," Lily said candidly. "That guy gives me the creeps. If I saw him walking toward me I'd run in the other direction."

"That's good," Doug said. "'Cause if he was walking toward you he'd be a zombie."

Everyone chuckled and then Jack put up Bobby Pickering's photos—first alive then after death. I found myself staring at the image of the crime scene I'd just left. The digital image on-screen couldn't capture what it had really been like. There was no face to visually identify Pickering, but it was the absence of blood spatter that kept me from being able to tear my eyes away from the photo. You could see where each of us had been standing because there was no blood in those spaces.

"First victim is David Sowers," Jack said. "He's got licenses to practice law in both Virginia and DC. He's got a shady past with a vehicular homicide that he was never charged for, he's got a thousand-dollar-a-day coke habit, and he likes underage girls. No military service or anything on the surface of his records that indicated he was affiliated with the military in any way. He and his current wife have lived in King George County since just after they married twelve years ago. I've got copies of his financials in this folder."

Martinez's brow arched suspiciously. "How'd you get those?"

Jack just smiled and kept talking. "On the surface, there's nothing unusual in his financials. He's got a healthy and diverse portfolio. But then you start peeling back the layers and you get to the shell companies, who own properties all over the world, with a high majority in Ukraine and

Malaysia, but these shell companies own a nice slice of the globe. Boarding houses most likely for their criminal activity. Succession plan states that remaining board members will split control of Sowers' shares."

"Who are the remaining board members?" Cole asked.

"Great question," Jack said. "Their names are hidden behind other shell companies. It's a tangled web that would even take Mackenzie some time to unravel."

"Challenge accepted," Mackenzie said. "I'm good at unraveling things. Sometimes when I'm watching the news I get curious and start poking around. Did you know that Anderson Cooper's underpants are hand sewn and every pair has his initials stitched in them?"

"You Carver boys would be in so much trouble if anyone really knows what you have in your possession," Cole said. "No wonder the FBI is sitting out in the street."

"No biggie," Doug said. "They're both playing games on their phones, and the lady agent is having an affair and texting her boyfriend and her husband. I keep waiting to see if she accidentally mixes them up."

"Lord have mercy," Jack said, dropping his head and massaging the back of his neck.

"Sometimes I'm amazed we all haven't gone to prison."

"Hey, we're the good guys," Martinez said. "Our methods are just a little unorthodox. Sometimes information just falls into our laps from an anonymous source. And what about the guy from today? Thanks for sending me to the alley, by the way. I really liked the shoes I was wearing. I would've had to throw them out."

"So sensitive," Lily said, slapping him lightly on the shoulder.

"Bobby Pickering," Jack said. "Who is thirty years younger than Sowers, has an exemplary military record with several commendations and was part of an elite special ops unit. He has no family ties to King George County but somehow landed here anyway. He works days at a construction company and weekends as a valet for extra cash. He basically has nothing in common with Sowers except that they were in the same location on a random Friday night.

"His name hasn't been mentioned in any of Sowers' client files," Cole said. "They'd wiped a lot of the computer files from the office, so IT didn't find anything mentioning Pickering, and it'll take time to go through the paper files. The tech guys have Pickering's phone and are looking for any numbers or contacts in Sowers' circle."

"Things on a computer are never really erased," Doug said. "If you'll bring me what was confiscated I can pull up any deleted files and see if there's a connection."

Cole looked at Jack and Jack nodded his permission.

"Whatever you and Mackenzie can pull out we'll be glad for it," Jack said, hitting another button on his computer. Images of Kateryna and Nia were placed on the board next.

"You know," I said thoughtfully. "Both of those women would certainly have a motive for killing Sowers."

Jack agreed. "Doug, let's do a deep background on both women. Check phone records, bank accounts. Let's see if they've ever had any contact. They're both victims, but maybe they got tired of being victims and decided to work together."

"Can't say I'd blame them if they did do it," Lily said.

"Which is why you're not a cop," Cole said, good-naturedly, squeezing her shoulders from behind.

The doorbell rang and Doug loped out of his chair and ran into the hallway, sliding on the wood floor and rebounding off the wall before answering the front door.

"Ahh, to have the energy and appetite of a sixteen-year-old," Cole said. "Those were the good old days."

"Excuse me," Lily said, putting her hands on her hips. "Your good old days haven't happened yet."

Cole shook his head and said, "That's easy to say when you can still eat pizza after six p.m. and not be up all night with heartburn."

"Old people problems mean more pizza for me," Doug said, coming back in the room with a stack of pizza boxes.

I went to the kitchen and grabbed paper plates and napkins, and then figured everyone had been to our house enough that they knew where the drinks were.

"How's it going, Mackenzie, love?" Doug asked when he settled back in his chair. "Find anything interesting?"

"Standard background check on both Kateryna Kovel and Nia Sowers complete," Mackenzie said. "That pizza smells delicious. If I had a body I could enjoy the same things the rest of you do."

"You know you can't smell, Mackenzie," Doug said. "You're just trying to guilt me into designing you a body. I told you I'm working on it with Uncle Ben. He's just a little busy right now."

Mackenzie *hmphh*ed in a very realistic and adult manner.

"Let's stay focused, okay," Doug said. "Can you display any relevant information on the board?"

"Your wish is my command, master," she said haughtily.

Doug rolled his eyes and he flushed with embarrassment.

The rest of us had gotten used to Mackenzie's hot temperament—at least as much as you could get used to a sarcastic and volatile non-being.

"Those are very tidy background checks," Cole said, scanning the information as it appeared on the board. "About as basic as you can get."

"That's what happens when you have a friend at the state department," Jack said. "They make things nice and tidy for some and then complicate the heck out of things for everyone else.

"Yeah," Martinez said around a bite of pizza. "Just ask anyone who was trying to bring down Jeffrey Epstein."

Jack's lips twitched, but he stayed focused. "Speaking of William Kirby, I'd like Mackenzie to run a deeper level check on him. Travel logs. Financials. Known associates."

"Skirting a line there, boss," Cole said. "None of it will be admissible without a warrant."

"You ain't seen nothing yet," Jack said. "Wait until I ask you to dig into military records."

"Ooh, I do love that man," Mackenzie said.

"Why does she suddenly sound like Mae West?" Cole asked.

"Who's Mae West?" Lily asked.

"You're killing me with the age thing," Cole said, shaking his head. "But I'm trying."

"Bring it down, Grandpa Joe," Martinez said. "Mae West was way before your time too. You wouldn't know who she was either if you didn't spend your off days watching AMC."

Mackenzie continued as if no one was talking. "It's nice when a man gives a woman a challenge. Isn't that right, Doug. A woman needs to be stimulated."

"Amen to that," Lily said.

"Ssh, don't encourage her," Cole whispered.

"What's happening here?" Jack asked. "I feel like I'm in the loony bin."

"They didn't take a nap like we did," I said, winking.

"Gross, is that sex talk?" Doug asked.

"No," I said. "When you get our age naps are important."

"Everyone in here knows they're not actually old, right?" Doug asked. "So weird."

"Hold up," Cole said. "Go back to what you were saying about military records."

"We'll never get a warrant on Kirby," Jack said. "We could have video of Kirby dancing on Sowers' skull holding the murder weapon, and we'd have to turn it over to the Justice Department. And then they'd bury it. It's what they do. Kirby knows he's protected because he didn't pull the trigger on Sowers. But anyone at the state department who's making diplomatic trips around the world would have access to the military. Or at least former military acting as private security. I want to see if Pickering was on assignment anywhere at the same time Kirby was visiting."

"I'm always happy to help you, Jack," Mackenzie purred, her voice changing to Kathleen Turner. "I'll run a scan now. I'll need Doug's assistance as there will be some obstacles considering this Kirby's position."

"Thank you, Mackenzie," Jack said. "Moving on." Jack hit a button on his laptop and Alex Denaro's face appeared on the wall. "Then we have an interesting fly in the ointment. I did a search on the Denaro family. His great-grandfather came from Italy in the forties and ran the mob in Little Italy in Philadelphia. They called him Big Lou, and then the torch was passed to the next generation after Big Lou's death.

"The whole thing sounds like a movie," he continued. "The Denaros have paid cops in their pockets and it's no secret who runs that part of town to this day. I don't know why Denaro left the organization—if he actually did—but he knew Sowers because he was a regular, and he knew about the drugs and women. And Bobby Pickering was his too. He was so helpful to give us his personnel file last night."

"Yeah," Martinez said, smirking. "I never trust anyone who seems too helpful. Everyone always has at least one thing to hide. Something that might not make them look so good."

"Cops are so weird," Lily said. "So you don't trust helpful people?"

"We don't really trust anyone," Martinez said. "Everyone lies."

"Sad," Lily said. "You need a good woman in your life."

He winked. "I've got plenty of good women in my life."

"Before Martinez can start reading off the names of the women in his phone," I said. "Why was there such a difference in the victim's head trauma this time? Was it a different weapon?"

"Same weapon," Jack said. "Different bullet. Not a hollow point this time. It was meant to destroy everything in its path. The killer wanted to make a scene and he got what he wanted. And maybe it was a warning."

"To who?" I asked.

"Maybe Darnell Watkins," Jack said. "Or maybe to us." And then he turned to Cole and Martinez. "What happened when you got Darnell into questioning?"

"He'd already lawyered up by the time we asked the first question," Martinez said. "Kid's scared to death."

"Who's the attorney?" Jack asked.

"Some guy named Rob Moretti," Cole said. "Looked like he came out of the Mafia playbook."

Jack raised his brows. "So maybe Alex Denaro has a reason for not wanting Darnell to talk. Did you get anything out of him?"

"Not one word," Martinez said. "Moretti wouldn't even let the kid say his name for the record. We can hold him for seventy-two hours, so that's what we'll do. Maybe he'll decide to start talking."

"Jail might be the safest place for him if the killer is knocking off people who could identify him," Jack said. "We'll give him a good night's sleep and then take another crack at him in the morning. He might be feeling real talkative."

"Those were our thoughts too," Cole said. "Kid's never been in trouble. Not even a parking ticket. A night in jail isn't going to sit well with him."

"I think Jaye and I need to pay a visit to Alex Denaro," Jack said.

CHAPTER TWELVE

THE WOMAN IN THE HOUSE ACROSS THE STREET from us had just recently been murdered by a copycat serial killer. Her house had been cleared of all the crime scene paraphernalia, but there was an eerie emptiness that accompanied the house now and the grass and weeds were starting to take over the front entryway.

I guess the agents figured the coverage was enough that their sedan wasn't visible, but we could see them parked as we came out of our gate and headed down Heresy Road. I resisted the urge to wave.

Alex Denaro and his wife had bought one of the old farmsteads not far from Jack's family land, so it didn't take us long to get there. Jack hadn't called first, so we were taking a chance that he'd be home. But it wasn't like he had a restaurant to open.

"Nice place," Jack said as we wound our way down a gravel drive.

The farmhouse was big and white, and there was a chicken coop that was a mini replica of the house off to one side. There was a big red barn back behind the house and a basketball goal in the driveway.

"Last thing I would've expected from a retired mobster," I said.

"That's why it's important not to stereotype," Jack said, parking the Tahoe in front of the house.

The porch lights were on and so were the lights in the front rooms. We could see the flicker of a television behind billowy white curtains as we walked up the porch steps. The front door cracked open before we were at the landing.

"Oh, it's you," Denaro said. He opened the door a little wider. "We're not used to getting visitors out here."

I could see the shotgun in his hand as he pushed open the screen door.

"We were hoping to catch you at home," Jack said. "Got a few minutes to talk?"

"Sure," Denaro said. "Come on in. The wife is upstairs giving the kids baths. I heard about

Bobby. Saw it all on the news. He was a good kid. Struggling I think with some PTSD. But he always showed up for work on time and was real friendly."

"Why'd you send the attorney for Darnell?" Jack asked.

Denaro smiled. "How'd you know he was mine?"

"I'm a cop," Jack said.

"Y'all come in here," Denaro said, leading us through the kitchen to a big farmhouse table. "It's quiet back here. Want something to drink?"

"No, we're good," Jack said, taking a seat at the table.

I took the chair beside him and Denaro sat across from us.

"I've known Moretti a long time," Denaro said. "And I know Darnell didn't have anything to do with any of this. He's barely twenty years old. He can't walk in a straight line without tripping over his own feet. There's no way he could be part of this."

"Then why would he be meeting Pickering?" Jack asked.

"I don't know," Denaro said. "You should ask him that."

"We tried, but your bulldog won't let him answer," Jack said.

Denaro grinned again, his square face expanding wide like a jack-o'-lantern. "Moretti is good, eh?"

"You've got to understand why we need to question you," Jack said. "You're right in the middle of this whole thing. You knew the victim and you employed our primary suspect, whom we never got to speak with. And you also employed the man he was meeting."

"You didn't mention my mob ties," Denaro said, his smile fading.

"I don't need to," Jack said. "Everything else is more than enough to question you on."

Denaro harrumphed. "I guess I can see how it would look coincidental from your end. But I didn't have nothing to do with nobody's death. Bobby was a good kid, and I'm sorry he's dead. I hope he wasn't involved. But the way I see it, it's probably not such a loss about the other guy."

"Did you know Bobby or Darnell before you hired them?" Jack asked.

"Nope," Denaro said. "I've got a connection at the construction company they all work at. He recommended both Bobby and J.D. and they came in to interview. And then Bobby was the one who recommended Darnell. I think they were living in the same apartment complex at the time and Bobby felt kind of sorry for Darnell.

Apparently he comes from a not so great home life. I like to help a guy out, so I gave him a job. Sue me."

"We appreciate the time," Jack said.

"Hey, anything I can do to help the law," Denaro said. "I'm a real supporter. Anything you need you let me know. And I'll tell Moretti to ease up on the kid. Darnell didn't have anything to do with any of this. I'd bet the farm on it."

———

"So now what?" I asked once we were back in the car.

"Now we go see if Darnell Watkins has had his fill of jail," Jack said. "I want to know why he was meeting Bobby Pickering."

"That's the million-dollar question," I said.

"When are you going to start the autopsy?" Jack asked.

"Tomorrow," I said. "There's no rush. We know cause of death. Did the forensics team find anything on Pickering's body?"

"There was a backpack under the table with a couple of thousand dollars in cash, two days' worth of clothes, and wait for it..."

"A new ID."

"Bingo," Jack said. "A shiny and new driver's license under the name of Beau Profit."

"Clever," I said. "I guess it's easiest to keep the initials the same."

"When you're running a con there's always a thread of truth in it somewhere. Speaking of William Kirby..." Jack hit the button on his steering wheel and asked to call Detective Cole. A few seconds later the phone was ringing.

"Boss," Cole said, answering the phone.

"Can you send me William Kirby's contact information?" Jack asked.

"Oh, sounds like I'm going to miss something fun," Cole said.

"A guy like Kirby is duty bound to help where he can," Jack said. "Surely he won't turn down an opportunity to smirk at us some more."

"Guys like that never do," Cole said.

"Found anything on your end?" Jack asked.

"Not anything significant," Cole said. "Martinez just got back with the electronics we confiscated from Sowers' office. Maybe we'll get lucky there."

"If the kid says he can do it, he can do it," Jack said. "Just keep him fed. I think the same rules apply to Doug as gremlins."

Cole chuckled and disconnected.

"What are you up to?" I asked.

"Just crossing my t's," he said. "Cole just texted Kirby's number." He handed me the phone. "Do me a favor and hit dial."

I typed in the number and then listened as the phone started ringing.

"William Kirby," Kirby said as he answered the phone.

"This is Sheriff Jack Lawson with the King George County Sheriff's Office," Jack said. "I'm sorry to interrupt your Saturday night."

"Not a problem," he said. "My wife and I are just about to leave to an event. I'm sure I have a few minutes before my wife finally decides to come downstairs."

He said it with good humor, a practiced politician.

"Well, I appreciate the time. We're trying to run David Sowers' shooter to ground."

"I'm honestly surprised the FBI hasn't taken over," Kirby said. "I've been watching the news about the latest victim. And from my understanding, there's a military connection to these murders. Seems like the scope is larger than what a small sheriff's department can handle."

Jack looked at me and raised a brow. There had been nothing in the news about our theory that the shooter might have been military, or even that Pickering had been in the military.

Which meant Kirby had gotten the information by some other means.

"It's always interesting to hear people's perceptions of what the FBI can and cannot do, but even you know they can't charge their way in and take over an investigation unless the killer crosses state lines. It's not their jurisdiction, and we have no plans of handing over the case."

"I've heard that about you," Kirby said. "I've done some digging. You're tenacious. Something of a bulldog. But your record and education are impressive. You'd be quite the asset to the government."

"I've been told that before," Jack said. "But my calling is here. I don't particularly like the red tape of federal law enforcement."

"Diplomacy calls for different avenues of investigating," Kirby said.

I almost snorted out a laugh. I'd never heard a quite so elegant turn of phrase for the corruption of federal law enforcement. There were plenty of good agents like Carver who were doing their best to protect and serve every day. Unfortunately, oil rises to the top.

"Did David Sowers ever need bodyguards on his trips overseas?" Jack asked.

"I've never been privy to David's business life," Kirby said apologetically. "Attorney client privilege. I've heard he was involved in some terrible things. It just goes to show how difficult it is to really know someone well."

"Did you ever use bodyguards or security when you travelled together?" Jack asked.

"I don't recall ever travelling with David," Kirby said. "I'm provided private transportation by the state department. I have military security once I land and then again at every US Embassy. And sometimes the embassy uses private contractors that have government contracts. I'm sorry I'm going to have to let you go. My wife just decided to make an appearance. We'll only be twenty minutes late."

"Would you mind meeting with me in the morning?" Jack asked. "My understanding is that you met regularly with Sowers and some of his employees. We have reason to believe someone close to him in that capacity might be involved."

"Of course," Kirby said agreeably. "Anything I can do for local law enforcement. It doesn't surprise me one bit. David's work environment was rather contentious. Especially with Jasmine Taylor. You should check her passport logs. I know for certain she's travelled with David before. I always suspected there was more to their relationship that met the eye."

"I'll look into it, sir," Jack said.

"I'll meet you in the morning," Kirby said. "There's a new breakfast place close to David's office I like. It looks like one of those outdoorsman stores."

"I know the one you're talking about," Jack said.

"Good. Ten o'clock. It'll give me a chance to make early mass." Kirby disconnected.

"Such an upstanding citizen," Jack said.

"What are you up to?" I asked.

"He's all ego," Jack said. "Kirby knows he can't be touched, so I figured he'd want to flaunt it as much as possible. I thought I'd dangle the carrot in front of him by suggesting his tablemates might have something to do with Sowers' murder, and he took the bite. He doesn't care that he's rolling on people he knew well enough to eat the occasional meal with. And now he feels like he's in control by setting up the time for the meeting and throwing me a bone by making it in my county. And what he's doing is *exactly* what I want him to do."

"That psychology is so sexy," I said.

"Obviously, that's why I got it," he said. "It serves no other purpose otherwise."

I grinned and tapped my fingers on the middle console.

"Where are we going?" I asked after we missed the turn to take us back toward home.

"I thought we'd give Darnell Watkins a chance to talk without his attorney."

"You realize we literally have nothing," I said. "No leads. Our main suspect is dead. And no ties between our victims. All we have is a killer who has some connection to them both and hasn't bothered to let us know what it is."

"Yeah," Jack said, his jaw clenching. "I know."

CHAPTER THIRTEEN

RETURNING TO THE SCENE OF THE CRIME WAS always a little surreal.

The glass had been swept away from the sidewalk and the windows were all boarded up. Even the neon purple sign had gone dark in solidarity. One of the streetlights flickered on the opposite side of the street and I could see the extra guards posted at the courthouse.

"Creepy," I said.

"Yeah," Jack said, pulling into his spot in front of the sheriff's office. "Definitely creepy. And bad for business."

Jack's phone rang just as he put the Tahoe in park, and an unknown number showed on the display screen.

"It's local," I said.

Jack sighed, internally debating whether or not to answer. Phone calls were rarely good news.

"Sheriff Lawson," Jack said.

"Yes, Sir," a male voice said. "This is J.D. Street. I'm a valet at the Purple Pig. You gave me your card last night."

"Sure, J.D. I remember you," Jack said. "What can I do for you?"

"I heard about Darnell on the news and that he'd been arrested," he said. "I wanted to see if there was anything I could do. Pay bail or something. I'm telling you there's no way that kid was any part of this. He's just young and dumb. I've been around awhile, and I've learned how to assess people quickly. He's good. And not just a little good. He's good to the depths of his soul. No way he'd hurt anyone or cause damage to someone's property."

"We're actually on our way to try and talk with him now," Jack said. "He's not been arrested so there's no bond. But he lawyered up so we can hold him for seventy-two hours."

"Lawyered up?" J.D. asked, the surprise evident in his voice. "That kid is so broke his bills have bills. No way he could afford a lawyer."

"Alex Denaro provided him with counsel," Jack said.

There was nothing but a heavy silence on the other end.

"You know why he'd do something like that?" Jack prodded.

"Mr. Denaro knows what he's about," J.D. said. "He must have thought Darnell needed a heavy hitter to help him out of this. Sorry to waste your time, Sheriff." And then he disconnected abruptly.

"Well, that was interesting," Jack said. "It's like everyone is privy to an inside joke and we're on the outside. I have to say I don't care for it."

"Welcome to my childhood," I said, smiling and then I exited the Tahoe.

I didn't know the night sergeant on duty when we walked into the sheriff's office. He was middle aged with a blond mustache, thinning hair, and his uniform seemed a little tight around the collar. There was a tan line on his ring finger.

"How's it going, Whipple?" Jack asked.

"Quiet night, sheriff," Whipple said. "Don't usually see you in this late. Everything all right?"

"Just tying up some loose ends," Jack said, and typed in the code to take us back to the bullpen.

The night shift lieutenant was at his desk in his office and Jack waved at him as we passed by. But the rest of the desks were empty. Jack didn't like his cops to spend their shifts sitting at their desks or hanging out in the squad room. He wanted them out in the streets. A visible police presence made citizens feel safe and criminals think twice about doing something stupid.

The smell of burned coffee was saturated into the carpet and walls, and there was an underlying smell of disinfectant. Someone had tried plugging in an oil diffuser but it just gave the coffee a slightly sick smell.

I followed Jack to a thick metal door that led to the holding cells, and watched as he typed in another code. The holding area wasn't real jail. It was where they brought those they were waiting to process or someone who was waiting on bail, and I figured Martinez and Cole left Darnell in holding because of his age and the fact that he'd never been in trouble before.

The cells were all empty except for the one on the end, and Darnell Watkins was sitting straight up on the narrow cot, his hands on his knees and his eyes on the blank wall in front of him.

"Darnell," Jack said, tapping his keys against the bar to get Darnell's attention. It was like he was in a trance. "It's Sheriff Lawson and Dr. Graves. You remember us?"

Darnell looked at us and nodded, his eyes

wide and unblinking. "I don't like it here. I want to go home. I didn't kill anyone. Bobby is dead."

Jack sighed and unlocked the cell door. "Let's go talk about this somewhere more comfortable."

"I can't stop seeing him die in my head," Darnell said. "He was right there. And then he wasn't. And then there was all that blood." He shuddered, and I knew exactly how he felt.

"I can give you the name of a good counselor who can help you with that," Jack said. "What you saw today is never easy."

"You've seen it before?" he asked.

"I have," Jack told him. "No one should have to experience that kind of trauma. But sometimes there isn't a choice. It's just what we do after the trauma that shapes the rest of our lives. Go to the counselor. Let him help."

"I don't have the money," Darnell said.

"You don't need any money," Jack said. "Dr. Gomez likes to help out the department. He'll help you too."

I knew that Jack would foot the bill for however long it took to get Darnell help, and he'd keep lying about the cost to save Darnell's pride.

"Okay, thanks," Darnell said.

I winced at the high-pitched squeak of the cell door as it opened.

"I'm not supposed to talk to anyone," he said.

"I'm supposed to call my attorney if someone tries to talk to me again."

"You can certainly do that," Jack said. "It's your right. But we can get you out of here much quicker if you tell us what you know. We just came from Alex Denaro's house. He was just trying to help you out with the attorney because he believes in you. All you have to do is tell us the truth."

Darnell let out a shaky breath. He was still in his street clothes—old jeans and a hoodie—and he got slowly to his feet. "All right. Do you think you can let me out if I tell you everything? I don't think I can spend the night here. I've never been in jail before."

"That's a good rule to live by," Jack said. "Let's hear what you have to say, and then we'll go from there. If you didn't do anything wrong then you've got nothing to hide."

Darnell nodded and we followed him out of the holding area and into an interview room. I wouldn't exactly call it more comfortable than the holding cell, but at least there wasn't a mattress and a toilet in sight. He sat in the single metal chair behind the metal table, and Jack and I took the two seats across from him.

Jack steepled his fingers together in front of him on the table. "When you and J.D. told us about Bobby last night, did you just suspect that he'd been the drive-by shooter or did you know for sure?"

"I just suspected," he said, shrugging. "Bobby was one of us. He was my friend. But I knew he had some dark places in him. Mr. Denaro said what he did in the war messed him up a little, so we're supposed to give him a break if he loses his temper or goes off by himself for a while. We kind of get used to it around here. Mr. Denaro likes hiring veterans. Says he feels like it makes amends for some of the stuff his family did."

"What stuff?" Jack asked.

"Mob stuff," Darnell said. "Mr. Denaro is really open about his past. He said we're all one big family here and families share the hard stuff. He's a really good boss."

"Uh-huh," Jack said.

"How many veterans does he have working for him?" I asked.

Darnell looked at me and I could see the wheels turning as he counted in his head. "I'm not sure, really. I mean, Bobby, and Kristina and Juan and Eddie—he works in the kitchen—and J.D. and Steven. There might be more, but I don't know all the servers real well."

"You mean J.D. and Steven the other valets?" I asked.

"Yeah," Darnell said, but then he paled slightly. "But don't go thinking bad of my boys. J.D. and I were hauling tail parking cars last night like we told you, and Steven was with his lady. That's why it was so weird when Bobby didn't show up. He was a nice guy. Always thinking about other people. Protective, you know? We thought he'd been shot, otherwise he would've been checking to make sure we were okay." He looked off to the side. "But he didn't."

Jack leaned back in his chair and I could tell something was starting to form in his mind. He had that look in his eye he got whenever something started to make sense. I didn't get that look in my eye. I was usually a step or two behind Jack.

"When did Bobby contact you?" Jack asked.

"After we left the restaurant last night," Darnell said. "I got back to my apartment after midnight, and then he called around one. Told me he had some important stuff to tell me, and he just had to get away last night after all the gunfire. I just figured it was some PTSD stuff, so I didn't think about it. I tried to ask him where he was during the shooting but he wouldn't let me talk. He said it was important I just listen. Then he told me to meet him at Heart Attack Burger and to come alone. The last place I wanted to drive was all the way across the county. Gas is expensive and I'm not real flush with cash right now."

"But you went anyway?" I asked.

"Sure," he said. "Bobby is...was a good guy. I wanted to help if I could. Whatever was going on with him."

"He didn't ask you to bring him anything?" Jack asked.

"Yeah," Darnell said, the question seemingly jogging his memory. "He asked if he could borrow my car for the day and a hundred bucks. He told me he'd bring the car back to my apartment before I had to go to work again."

"That's all he asked for?" Jack asked.

"Yeah," Darnell said. "I was just helping a guy out. No big deal. I mean, obviously Bobby wasn't the one who killed that guy at the restaurant. Bobby's dead now too."

"We appreciate your cooperation, Darnell," Jack said. "You can sit here and we'll get the paperwork started for your release. You can go home tonight."

"Really?" Darnell asked.

"Really," Jack said. "You're a good kid. Keep doing the right thing."

"What do you think?" I asked as we headed back home.

"About what specifically?" Jack asked.

"You had one of those lightbulb moments when you were talking to Darnell," I said. "What gives?"

"I want to take a closer look at the employees at the Purple Pig," Jack said. "It seems like a ripe hunting ground for someone with those kinds of sniper skills. Maybe Kirby's frequent visits had more to do someone else than they had to do with David Sowers and the gang."

"It's getting late," I said. "Who else do you want to talk to?"

"I'd like to pay another visit to Jasmine Taylor," Jack said. "She seemed to work the closest with Sowers. And it was obvious from the last time we talked to her that she knows things she doesn't want anyone else to know. Maybe she's close by. Look her up in the computer and if she's on the way we'll stop in."

I angled his computer toward me and typed in Jasmine Taylor's name. "You'd be surprised how many Jasmine Taylors there are in the county."

"Narrow it down by age and race," he said.

"Right, got it," I said. "She's got a Bloody Mary

address. Actually, she lives in the building next to Kateryna. Convenient."

Jack snorted and did a U-turn in the street to head back toward the Towne Square where we'd just come from.

The building next to Kateryna's was slightly different in style—federal-style row houses—each one painted in a bright color. Each building had a private door and stoop that faced the street and a black iron plate with the house number to the right of the door. Jasmine Taylor lived in the third row house.

There was parking directly in front of her yellow townhome, and her porch lights were on. The street was quiet—the whole downtown was quiet—probably due to everyone being scared to venture out. It was a different experience knowing someone could be lying in wait with a rifle in their hands.

Planters flanked both sides of her doors, but the flowers had died and weeds sprouted haphazardly. The welcome mat was plain and there was no wreath on the red door, only a simple knocker. All in all, it felt like a home whose homeowner was too busy to tend to it.

I jolted at the sight of the old Victorian turn doorbell. I'd grown up with a similar one, and I'd always hated the sound. Jack turned the key and what sounded like a cat getting its tail stepped on echoed from inside the house.

The front door opened and Jasmine Taylor stood in the crack, blocking our view to the inside of the house.

"I've already talked to the police," she said. "Twice. I've got nothing more to add."

She started to close her door, but Jack wedged his foot in the space. She glanced around us up and down the street and I saw the fear in her eyes. She didn't want anyone to see her talking to the police.

"Just a few follow-up questions. We've got two people dead, so we have to keep tracking down leads."

"Fine," she said. "I'll give you five minutes. After that you'll need to talk to my attorney. Come inside."

She led us into the foyer and no farther. It was painted a soft yellow with white trim and there was a bench and shelves against the wall with a briefcase, a pair of sneakers and an umbrella lying on the bench. I stepped onto a woven multicolor rug that reminded me of my grandmother, and there was a narrow white staircase that led to a darkened floor above.

"An attorney with an attorney," Jack said. "I've never met an attorney who didn't want to represent themselves. Is there anything you need an attorney for?"

"Coming here and insulting me isn't going to get you the information you want," she said.

"I'm not too worried about that," Jack said. "I'm not here to make friends. You've committed professional suicide working for David Sowers. As long as he was alive everyone associated with him could keep his dirty little secrets quiet. But now that he's dead you're seeing your name on the national news. That's got to suck."

"I haven't heard a question yet," she said. "Three minutes left."

"The thing about electronics is they can never be completely wiped," Jack said. "There's always a residue that's left. The hard part of this case is finding out who wanted to kill Sowers. And Bobby Pickering. It seems they were both tied up with the trafficking."

She flinched and Jack pressed harder.

"Yeah, you know all about that, don't you?" Jack asked. "You watched him bring these young girls back. You knew every time he left on a trip what he was going to do. Yet you continued to work for him. Maybe you liked it. We're already digging into your financials. I can't wait to see what we're going to find there."

"You can't do that without a warrant," she said, eyes narrowing.

"We have one," Jack said, and handed her a folded piece of paper. "Your bank has already been served. They're cooperative."

"Time's up," she said, and walked back to the front door, but not before I could see the fear on her face.

We followed, but slowly. "You know," Jack said. "William Kirby mentioned your name. He's coming in to talk with us in the morning. Isn't it funny how it's always the low-level players that take the fall for the big guys?"

Her eyes narrowed. "Kirby mentioned my name?"

"You specifically," Jack confirmed.

"That bastard," she hissed.

"Whoever our killer is obviously has his own warped sense of justice," Jack said. "Snipers always have a kill list. I wonder who else is on it."

She opened the door and then closed it quickly behind us. We heard the deadbolt click with finality.

"Feel better?" I asked.

"A little," he said. "There's more to her than meets the eye."

"Bad?" I asked. "You think she's more involved in this than we think?"

"I don't know. She's got layers. Maybe Doug can dig something up on her." He opened the door of the Tahoe for me and helped me in, and then he went around to his side. I saw him look up and down the street before he got in.

"What are you looking at?" I asked.

"Our FBI friends," he said. "They must have a tracker on the car. Let's go home and see what the guys have found out. It's going to be a long night."

"You know they've already eaten all the food," I said. "Better stop by and pick something up."

"You just want tacos," he said.

"Now that you mention it," I said. "I wouldn't mind a snack. You could buy our FBI friends some while you're at it. It humors me to think of taco droppings falling on their fancy suits."

CHAPTER FOURTEEN

EVERY LIGHT IN THE HOUSE WAS ON WHEN WE GOT back home.

"I was surprised they took the tacos," I told Jack, looking back at the agents who were making themselves at home in our neighbor's driveway again.

"They must have been hungry," Jack said.

"You should've told them how super helpful they were today when Pickering got his brains blown out on us."

"Who do you think made the anonymous 911 call?" Jack asked. "The FBI isn't as exciting as most people think. Every person there is neatly filed into a box, and they don't perform outside of their function. These guys are just drones. Their only assignment is to follow us around and make sure we're not communicating with the Carvers. They'll eventually get called to another assignment when they realize there's nothing for them here."

I could hear the television blaring some kind of sports when we walked in and then Doug skidded into the hallway.

"I smelled food," he said, taking the bags of tacos from Jack's hands. "We're starving. Y'all have nothing to eat here."

"That's because you keep eating it all," Jack said.

"I'm growing into my feet," Doug said. "At least that's what my mom says. She really appreciates y'all letting me live here by the way."

When we went into the office Cole was standing in front of the whiteboard in thought and Martinez was reading documents at the conference table. Lily had fallen asleep on the couch in front of the fire. The basketball game was on the TV, but no one was watching it."

"How'd it go?" Cole asked. "You got Darnell to talk?"

"Didn't take much," Jack said. "He's not meant for a life of crime. Pickering had called him and asked to borrow his car and a hundred bucks. Darnell was just in the wrong place at the wrong time with the wrong friends."

"That's how it usually starts," Cole said.

"I made a call to Kirby," Jack said.

"Ballsy," Martinez said. "I like it. What'd he say?"

"Super helpful in his narcissism," Jack said. "He's suspicious of Jasmine Taylor. He was happy to cast shade her way. And of course, he's heard on the news about all the terrible things Sowers was involved in. But he's willing to meet with us in the morning and help however he can."

"I really don't like that guy," Cole said. "Why bother meeting with him?"

"Because he might let something slip," Jack said. "The world of trafficking is vast, but the circles are small. A guy like Kirby is established at the state department, but I guarantee he's not involved anyone in his work environment in his extracurricular activities. But he's in a position to have a lot of international contacts. He's out of the country more than he's in the United States. He'll have an established team. And then he'll have lower-level guys like Sowers and maybe Jasmine Taylor who are expendable, or who could take the fall if things get too hot."

"Speaking of Kirby's travel logs," Martinez said. "This guy is all over the place. And if you compare his travel to Sowers, there are some overlying patterns. They never arrive or depart on the same day. They might spend a day, at the most two, in the same city at the same time. I've got twenty-one occurrences over the last five years. I haven't gone back any further."

"Sowers' widow knew about Kirby," I said. "She pretended she didn't, but she was lying. There's no telling how far back Kirby and Sowers have been involved in this."

"Well," Doug said, "I've already connected William Kirby to one of the shell companies you gave me that David Sowers has been using. There are five members total on the board. My guess would be they're on the boards of every company, but it's slow going to peel back the layers. Mackenzie has to be very delicate so she doesn't set off alarms. We don't want to end up back under house arrest."

"Can you do a deep run on Jasmine Taylor?" Jack asked.

"Sure," Doug said. "I can do it manually while Mackenzie is working. What am I looking for?"

"Any glitches in her identity or credentials," Jack said. "She hasn't been working for Sowers that long. Just over two years. That in itself makes me suspicious that she was able to work herself into his network so quickly."

"Maybe the cocaine addled his brain," Cole said.

"Maybe," Jack said. "Or maybe she's working undercover."

"For who?" Martinez asked.

"I don't know," Jack said. "But she's not a stupid woman. Her file says she's a Harvard graduate, just like Sowers. Attaching herself to Sowers would be career suicide, and she'd know that. She's sat on national boards and has taught classes at the university. And four years ago she was tapped to sit on the president's legal team. From what I can tell, she's taken on most of the legal duties in the office since Sowers' drug use made him unreliable. The trafficking might have been shoved under the rug, but it seems everyone knew about the drugs, and has known for a long time."

"So what am I looking for specifically?" Doug asked. "If she's working undercover with a fake ID, I could hack into the database. They have a separate system for undercover licenses."

"I think she's using her real identity," Jack said. "Look at her training. I watched her the first time we met at the Purple Pig and then tonight. The way she kept distance between herself and us. The way she stood and angled her body."

"Oh," Cole said. "I see it now."

"Someone want to explain to me since I don't see?" I asked.

"She moves like a cop," Jack said. "That's all law enforcement training. The way she was constantly scanning the area instead of making eye contact. And she was wearing a weapon in the small of her back tonight."

"She did eighteen months at Quantico after law school," Doug said.

"So my guess is she's connected with the attorney general's office and the DOJ," Jack said. "They'd have put her in the right places at the right times so she'd spark Sowers' notice, and she'd still be able to use her real name. Anything come up on Alex Denaro?"

"He appears to have turned over a new leaf," Martinez said. "I was just going through his financials. He's part owner in a couple of different businesses. Makes a healthy income, but not crazy. Wife stays home with the kids. Has a mortgage. Pays taxes. Seems on the up and up."

"What businesses?" Jack asked.

"Umm..." Martinez said, shuffling through papers. "A shipping container yard in King George Proper near the docks. And Miller Construction. He's listed as a fifty percent owner in both."

"Who's the other owner?" I asked.

"Louis Giordano," Martinez said.

Doug typed on his keyboard with lightning speed. "Looks like Giordano is a cousin. His mother was a Denaro."

"So maybe he's not as far removed from the family business as he wants us to believe," Jack said. "Okay, we know the big players in this. Or potential big players if Denaro is involved. Let's bring it down a level and look for the workmen. Denaro makes it a habit of hiring veterans. According to Darnell, there's at least five or six who are employed in some capacity. Do we have Denaro's employee list?"

"Right here," Martinez said, shuffling papers. "And copies of his personnel files. He's a real helpful guy."

"I know," Jack said. "Color me suspicious. Let's pull them up on the computer and put them on the screen."

Martinez took the files and moved to Jack's desk to sit behind the computer there.

"You know Mackenzie could do that for you?" Doug said.

"I know," Jack said. "But I like to justify paying everyone to the taxpayers. Besides, Mackenzie has enough on her plate."

"Thank you, Jack," Mackenzie said. "I am a little overwhelmed at the moment. It's nice when someone thinks of my well-being and doesn't just think of his own needs."

"Kid's got a lot to learn about women," Cole said, shaking his head.

"What did I do?" Doug asked, raising his hands.

"Exactly my point," Cole said.

"Here we go," Martinez said, before things between Doug and Mackenzie could deteriorate. "Kristina Hendricks. Age twenty-four. Did four years in the army and was honorably discharged. Looks like she's a student at KGU. Been employed with Denaro since he opened as part of his wait staff. Looks like she's still living with her parents."

"Okay, we won't rule her out, but she doesn't fit the profile," Jack said. "Let's go ahead and run financials on all of these guys. And when Mackenzie has a chance I want to see their military records."

"I'll start a side search," Mackenzie said.

"Thank you," Jack told her.

"You're welcome, Jack," Mackenzie said in a tone that had my brows rising.

"Careful, Mackenzie," Jack said. "Jaye will come after you."

Her laughter was throaty and seductive. "Sorry, Dr. Graves. You're a lucky woman."

"Yes," I said. "Though I wonder what chance I'd have if you had a body to go with that voice."

"None at all," Mackenzie said definitely, making me burst with laughter.

"I will never get used to this," I said.

"This is the future," Doug said.

"That's my concern," I told him. "Do humans exist in the future, or does Mackenzie take over?"

"Is that a hypothetical question?" Mackenzie asked. "Or am I supposed to answer?"

"It's probably best left unanswered," Jack said.

"Whatever you say, darling," she said. "I have the information on Jasmine Taylor if you'd like me to put it on the screen."

"Thank you, Mackenzie," Jack said. "Please do."

"You called that one," Cole said, reading Jasmine Taylor's information from the board. "They really do have terrible cyber security. Looks like she's on assignment from the DOJ. Do you think she's investigating Sowers or Kirby?"

"That's the million dollar question, but not our problem, thank God," Jack said. "Let's keep looking at the veterans on staff at the Purple Pig."

"Next is Juan Ramirez," Martinez said. "He's also on wait staff. Age thirty-three. Did twelve years in the navy. Honorably discharged. Married to Gina Hernandez Ramirez. Two kids and another on the way. He's been with Denaro about six months. Looks like he's a firefighter at station three. I'm guessing he waits tables on his off days.

"Next is Eddie Lische," Martinez said. "Also did four years in the army and is a student at KGU. Honorable discharge. Age twenty-five."

"That's a connection between him and Kristina," Jack said. "Same branch of the service. Around the same age. Same college campus."

"Looks like he's living in an on-campus apartment with a couple of roommates," Martinez continued. "And then there's Bobby Pickering. We're just waiting on financials for him."

"What about the other valets?" Jack asked. "Darnell mentioned they were veterans."

"Yeah, umm," Martinez said, squinting and putting up two more photographs on the board. "J.D. Street and Steven Machilenski. Wow, is that a mouthful."

"We met J.D. the night of the shooting," Jack said. "Steven is the one who called in sick, but both J.D. and Darnell said they thought he wasn't sick but with his girlfriend."

"Steven Machilenski," Martinez said. "Marines."

"Just like Pickering," Jack said.

"But get this," Martinez continued. "He's got a

dishonorable discharge and a court-martial for going AWOL on his record. Employed at Miller Construction. Lives in King George Proper."

"Which ties it all back to Denaro," Jack said, squeezing the bridge of his nose. "But that does make things more interesting. What about J.D.?"

"J.D. Street," Martinez said, reading from his file. "Thirty-four years old. Air force. Has some commendations and combat experience. Did ten years and then after an honorable discharge moved to Florida to join Dynamo—a private contracting firm. Looks like he did some private contracting for them overseas for a couple of years before he came back and became a regular citizen. His mission files there will be sealed. Dynamo has better security than Fort Knox."

"Challenge accepted," Doug said.

Martinez grinned. "Street is a contract manager now for Miller Construction. Single. Has a house in Nottingham. Has a mortgage and a car payment. And court documents show he has a twelve-year-old son in South Carolina. He's up to date on child support."

Cole had been quiet over at the end of the conference table on his own laptop, but I saw him prop his boots on the corner of the table and knew he'd found something.

"I've got financials open for Kristina

Hendricks and Eddie Lische," Cole said. "Both of them had a one-time deposit of two thousand dollars in January."

"Who's it from?" Jack asked.

Cole smiled and said, "Alex Denaro."

CHAPTER FIFTEEN

I WASN'T NORMALLY THE KIND OF PERSON WHO could wake up without an alarm clock or the scintillating aroma of coffee, but I found myself wide awake before the sunrise was even a hint in the sky. I knew we were getting closer to finding our killer.

"I can hear your mind churning," Jack said. "Why are you awake?"

"Why are you awake?" I countered.

"Because my mind is churning too," he said. "How early is too early to start questioning people? I know we're close. I can feel it."

"And if only we could somehow bring William Kirby down it would be the cherry on top," I said.

"Yeah, I have half a mind to cancel just to

annoy him," Jack said. "We know he's guilty of trafficking. We have an eyewitness. But we can't do anything about it, and unfortunately we can't arrest him for murder. He's basically meeting with us to rub his misdeeds in our faces."

I snorted. "Misdeeds," I mocked. "How dastardly."

I laughed as his fingers tickled my ribs, and somehow we managed to fill the next hour before Jack's alarm went off.

Cole had scooped up Lily and taken her home sometime after two in the morning, and Martinez had followed them out. We'd all agreed to start early the next morning with new assignments. Cole was going to meet with Denaro about the money found in Kristina Hendricks's and Eddie Lische's bank accounts. Martinez would track down Hendricks and Lische to question them since we'd already found out neither of them had been at work on the night Sowers was killed at the Purple Pig. And that left Jack and me to question Steven Machilenski and see if he had an alibi since he called in sick for work.

"I'll admit," I said after we'd showered. "I kind of like Alex Denaro. I really didn't want it to be him."

"Don't paint him completely guilty just yet,"

Jack said. "There's a lot of moving parts and players in this."

"But you think he's involved?"

Jack sighed and pulled out a denim shirt with the sheriff's office logo over the breast pocket. "It doesn't look good for him right now."

"You're looking very official for the weekend," I said, watching him pull a black sweater over the denim shirt. The sweater also had the sheriff's office logo over the heart and on the left sleeve. He pulled on a pair of jeans and a black belt and his boots. "And you are also looking entirely too sexy to be going out in public like that."

He grinned and winked at me and then he put on his duty belt and grabbed his nice black suede coat from the closet. I'd never seen him wear that coat to work.

"Kirby's a narcissist and he's always going to want to be better and seem smarter than everyone else. We're going to disappoint him today. The Lawson name and money comes in handy from time to time. Wear the black boots with the red soles and this too," he said, pulling out a black suit that still had the tags on it.

"I have an autopsy to do today," I said.

"You can change beforehand," he said. "This is strictly for Kirby's benefit. We'll stop by Machilenski's place, and then head over to the restaurant to meet Kirby. You'll barely have time to get it dirty."

"Easy for you to say," I told him. "There's a reason I don't wear expensive clothes on a day-to-day basis. Even my funeral suits are durable and washable. This outfit seems like neither of those things."

Jack laughed. "You're a grown woman. You're going to be fine. Now get dressed and let's roll."

Jack went down to make coffee and I touched the sleeve of the jacket. Definitely not washable. But I put on the clothes anyway, surprised how comfortable they were. Apparently silk really did breathe.

After I got dressed, I realized I looked too nice to not do something more with my face than just put on moisturizer, so spent a few minutes on my eyes, surprised how much they popped with a little shadow and mascara, and then I put on lipstick I was sure to chew off within a couple of hours. Satisfied with the outcome, I headed downstairs.

I was surprised to see Doug in the kitchen. He wasn't an early riser by any means.

"Whoa," he said, looking at me. "Are y'all in some sexiest couple alive contest?"

"Yes," Jack said deadpan.

"What are you doing up so early?" I asked,

taking my to-go cup from Jack. I took a moment to inhale the aroma before testing to see how hot it was. No one made coffee like Jack.

"Haven't been to bed yet," Doug said. "It's taken all night to get those military records. I know Uncle Ben could've done it faster, but I wanted to make sure I didn't lead anyone back here. We're good though. Mackenzie is almost through and then we'll be able to see if anyone's assignments overlapped and specialized skill sets. We'll also be able to match with Kirby's and Sowers' international travel. State department has crap security, so I was able to get in there easily and get all his information."

"Be careful," Jack said.

"I'm always careful," Doug said, opening the refrigerator. Nothing had magically appeared since the night before, so he closed it and went to the pantry to get the bread. He put a couple of slices in the toaster and then got out the butter and grape jelly.

"You know what's interesting though," Doug said after a few minutes. "The FBI has a file on David Sowers. They have one on Kirby too."

Jack put down his coffee cup with an audible *thunk* and his gaze narrowed on Doug.

"No," Jack said. "We do not need the FBI to come down on us right now. You don't think they're looking for any breaches or abnormalities in security now that Carver is out? Stay out of the FBI database. I don't care how important the information is. You're not going to find anything to help your uncle by doing it that way."

Doug's expression went sullen and he said, "I can't just sit here and do nothing. Uncle Ben always says that information is the most important commodity we as citizens have."

"Yes, and people die with information that never sees the light of day all the time," Jack said. "Your Uncle Ben is the most brilliant man I've ever known. The FBI is scared to death of him. Because they know that in the end he'll be able to outsmart and outgun them. And a lot of people are going to go down for it. Make no mistake, anyone looking for your Uncle Ben right now doesn't care about containing him. They want to kill him. Whatever he's got is that valuable. Let him do what he does best. If he needs help he'll ask for it. Promise me that."

"Yeah, fine," Doug said, putting more bread in the toaster. The loaf would be gone before we got back home.

"If you and Mackenzie find out anything interesting give me a call," Jack said. "Call, don't text."

"Got it," Doug said. And then he grinned. "A

hundred bucks Jaye comes home dirty and that suit is ruined for life."

"Have a little faith," Jack said and grabbed his keys.

I slung my medical bag over my shoulder and followed Jack out. And then I turned to Doug. "Not even I would take that bet."

We were running a little behind by the time we got on the highway and were headed toward King George. Our FBI friends were behind us, not even bothering to keep a couple of car lengths between us anymore.

"Guess they want more tacos," I said. "Where are we going?"

"The apartments off of Seabury," Jack said.

I grimaced. "Bad part of town. If Pickering was asking Darnell for money and his car, it seems pretty obvious he was planning to skip down. Steven would probably do the same."

"Only if he's guilty," Jack said, turning onto Seabury.

The trees and grass were overgrown around trailers in different states of disrepair. There were tires and old cars missing parts parked in yards, along with various appliances that had seen better days. At the end of the block was a three-story apartment building.

We passed a patrol unit as we pulled into the parking lot and Jack said, "I've always got units patrolling out here. We get a high volume of calls from this area and the police presence helps keep things at a minimum."

"Makes sense," I said, looking down at my suit and shoes and then glancing at the potholed parking lot.

Jack pulled right in front of the entrance and turned his lights on, but he left his sirens off.

"Lots of drugs move through here, and lots of junkies. We routinely have to roust the empty apartments for the landlord so he can rent them out."

I saw the flutter of a few curtains as faces peeked to see what was going on, and then like rats, they scurried away.

Jack opened the door for me and I stepped into a dingy lobby with oppressive heat and gray threadbare carpet. The heater rumbled and spat and poured from the vents above, and my skin was damp with sweat in seconds. Several rows of mailboxes sat to the right side, and there was a single elevator to the left with a sign taped to it that said *Use the Stairs*.

"Of course," I said.

Jack grunted. "And he lives on the third floor."

"Even better. Heat rises."

Jack led the way up the stairs, his hand resting on his weapon. The heat became more oppressive as we climbed higher. We didn't see a single person and didn't hear a peep. It was as if we had the whole building to ourselves.

"Where is everyone?" I asked.

"The people who live here get really good at disappearing when the cops show up."

"This wasn't what I was expecting after hearing Darnell talk about Steven the other night. He said Steven has a girlfriend. No girlfriend would come here. It would be hard to live here and then keep the façade that everything is normal at work."

"Maybe he stays with the girlfriend," Jack said. "We'll see if we can track her down too. Darnell mentioned Pickering suffered from PTSD and that he'd go off on his own sometimes or lose his temper. Maybe Steven struggled too. He serves his country and comes back home and nothing is the same. He's still young, but he feels old. He works at the construction company in the day and the restaurant at night, and if he works enough hours then he doesn't have time to think about the bad things. He doesn't care about where he sleeps because he's hardly ever there. He probably has a girlfriend on a regular basis because that's someone who can occupy the hours he's not working."

"Sad," I said.

"It is," Jack agreed. "And all too common. This is just a flophouse. He probably has little, if any, personal belongings."

By the time I made it to the top my hair was damp with sweat and I was sucking in as much air as I could through my mouth so I didn't have to smell through my nose. The floor squeaked beneath our feet, and I could hear the low rumble of a television behind the first door we passed by. Steven's apartment was at the end of the hall.

"Apartment 3F," Jack said as we approached.

The television across the hall was loud enough to hear word for word and sing along with the insurance jingle, but I slowed my steps as we approached 3F. The smells of overcooked food and disrepair morphed into something I was all too familiar with.

"Jack," I said.

"Yeah, I smell it," he said, and pulled his weapon from his holster and put it down at his side. Then he rapped on the door directly across the hall loud enough that whoever was inside could hear over the television.

He waited a couple of seconds and then used his fist to pound again.

The door opened and a scrawny rooster of a man who looked to be on the better side of seventy jerked the door open. He wore a dingy wifebeater and a pair of gray cargo pants that had the top button undone.

"What?" he yelled. "I'm watching my shows."

Jack pulled out his badge. "The guy across the hall. When was the last time you saw him?"

"Who knows? I don't keep tabs."

"Any visitors? Any fights?"

"There's always visitors and fights in this place. Not my business. There's a reason I keep my TV up so loud."

"You haven't noticed the smell?" Jack asked incredulously.

"Always smells like a piss pot in here," he said. And then he slammed the door shut.

"Seems like a nice guy," I said, pulling on a pair of gloves.

Jack rolled his eyes and then knocked loudly on Steven Machilenski's door. There was no sound from inside. We hadn't expected one.

"Try the door," Jack said.

I reached for the doorknob and rattled it, but

it was locked. The door and lock were flimsy at back, so Jack signaled for me to move to the side and then kicked right where the locking mechanism was. The doorframe splintered and the door slammed open.

The smell was even stronger now and I waited for Jack to go in before slipping behind him. We stepped inside a dim one-room apartment. There was a small kitchenette to the side and a single window with a sheet nailed over it. But there was enough light filtering in so we could see the body sitting in the chair.

"I'm going to guess that's Steven Machilenski," I said.

Jack walked the perimeter of the room and checked the bathroom and closet, but there was no one else there.

"You were right," I said. "Nothing personal here. The kitchen cabinets are clean. There's no dirty dishes." I opened the refrigerator. "No food at all. No family pictures. Just a TV, a recliner, and a mattress on the floor. Actually, it seems remarkably clean compared to the rest of the building."

I could smell the underlying scent of Pine-Sol beneath the decomposition.

Jack put his weapon away and took out his phone to call it in, and I moved closer to the body. I'd seen his picture and read his profile the night before. There was a single GSW to the right temple.

"Small caliber," I said. "Enough to get the job done and not make a complete mess. There's no exit wound."

"Team is on the way," Jack said, and studied the body. "He pulls the trigger, it kicks his hand back, and then the gun drops to the floor."

I stared at the angle of the arm and the weapon on the carpet just beneath it. "Yeah, and gunshot residue around the wound." I picked up the victim's wrist and looked closer. "Also visible residue on the thumb and index finger. All consistent with suicide."

I looked at Jack and knew what that meant. Usually when a suicide like this occurred it was because there was guilt involved.

"He doesn't smell of alcohol," I said. "No evidence of drugs or alcohol in the apartment."

"What's that?" Jack asked, leaning across Steven and pointing to a piece of paper wedged between him and the seat.

I handed Jack a pair of gloves and he put them on before gingerly pulling a piece of paper from beneath the victim's other arm.

"Suicide note," he said.

I raised my brows in surprise. "Well, that

makes things more interesting. What does it say?"

Despite movies and television portraying the contrary, the majority of suicides didn't actually leave a note.

Jack read aloud.

I'm sorry. I thought I was helping. I thought I was doing the right thing. I killed Bobby. We thought he could handle it like soldiers do. But he couldn't. I don't belong here. It's better this way.

"He's confessing to killing Bobby," I said, looking at Jack.

Jack nodded, already knowing where I was going. "But not to Sowers. Two shooters. Two different kinds of bullets used. But all of them involved in whatever is going down. What's your estimation on time of death?"

"He's in full rigor," I said. "So that gives us a window of at least twelve hours to sixteen hours. Bobby Pickering was shot around noon yesterday. So we're probably looking at anywhere between one to six or seven o'clock."

I heard the sirens approaching. I reached for an evidence bag and held it open for Jack to put the letter inside.

"You know what else is missing?" Jack asked.

I looked at him blankly.

"There's no weapon."

CHAPTER SIXTEEN

"We're going to be late meeting with Kirby," I said, looking at my watch.

"Did you know that thirty-seven percent of all meetings start late?" Sheldon asked.

"I did not know that," I said.

"That's because everyone secretly knows most meetings are a colossal waste of time and can be done from the comfort of your computer screen at home," Lily chimed in.

"My mother does that," Sheldon said. "She thinks it's funny that no one knows she's not wearing pants."

I ducked my head to hide my smile. Cops were knocking on every door in the building to see if someone could tell them if they'd heard a shot fired or seen anyone with Steven Machilen-ski. The forensic techs were combing the room, and Jack was in the parking lot searching for Steven's car.

"I'm finished with my cursory report and I have all the photographs I need," I told Lily. "You guys are good to transport him back to the funeral home. As soon as I'm done with Kirby I'll be in and we can start on the autopsies."

"Umm..." Sheldon said, raising his hand. "We have a guest coming in this afternoon as well. Edna Dryer. Her daughter said she wants the full package."

"Oh, yeah," I said. "I knew Edna. She's from Bloody Mary. I went to school with her grand-daughter. Edna used to run all the bake sales at the Methodist church. She'd always give us a piece of coffee cake when we'd ride by on our bikes. I don't know how the church made any money."

"That's sweet," Lily said. "She's not supposed to arrive until sometime after two, so we should be through with Pickering before she arrives."

I nodded and said, "Sheldon can take point on Edna. I want to get these autopsies out of the way. We're closing in on the right person. I can feel it. I'm going to head out and see if I can find

Jack. I'm interested to see if Kirby knows any of our dead soldiers."

I trusted Lily and Sheldon to get the body back to the funeral home, so I exited the hallway as fast as I could, my only focus to draw in fresh air and escape the stifling heat.

I met Jack on the way down the stairs.

"You're in a hurry," he said, turning around to follow me back down.

"I've had my fill of overheated corpse," I said. "I notice you didn't come back upstairs."

"To give myself credit," he said, smiling, "I was on my way back up to get you."

"You should've taken Doug's bet," I told him, letting the cold air slap against my face. "I haven't gotten a spot on me. I'm only a little wilted."

"And as long as Kirby doesn't get too close he won't smell either one of us," Jack said, making me wince.

"Well, hopefully it'll be a short meeting," I said.

"We found Steven's car, but there was no weapon inside," Jack said. "We did find a few loose rounds in his back seat. And guess what he drives?"

"A white sedan?" I guessed.

"Bingo."

We got into the Tahoe, and I rolled down the window, still in need of fresh air. And maybe enough to air us both out.

"I also heard back from Cole," Jack said. "Denaro told him the two thousand dollars were scholarships to help Kristina Hendricks and Eddie Lische with anything extra they needed for school or housing that the GI Bill didn't cover. Martinez said that checked out with what Hendricks and Lische told him too."

"So maybe Denaro isn't involved," I said thoughtfully.

The Big Over Easy was in the middle of King George Proper, not far from the university. Kirby had been right when he said it looked like one of those extreme outdoorsman stores. It was two stories of dark timber, river rock, and glass, and it was a popular hangout for kids from the college.

"Why am I nervous?" I asked.

"Maybe because he's a horrible man who traffics young girls?"

"It's weird," I said. "I feel like I'm on a job interview. Maybe it's the clothes."

"And we're only five minutes late."

"Thirty-seven percent of all meetings start late," I said, parroting Sheldon.

"Very helpful statistics for this situation," Jack said. "Come on."

The place was packed when we walked in, and there was a waiting list started. Breakfast time on a Sunday morning was not the best time to go to a popular restaurant.

"Sheriff Lawson," a young woman said, coming over to us quickly. "Mr. Kirby is already waiting for you upstairs. We're really honored to have you both here at The Big Over Easy. My name's Carissa, and I'm the manager. Please let me know if there's anything you need."

Jack had never been one to use his position to get special favor or privilege, but it seemed like Kirby had no problem throwing his weight around.

Jack's phone rang and he looked at the screen, showing me it was Doug on the line. "Let me take this really quick. It's important."

"Of course," Carissa said and turned to me. "I can take you up if you'd like."

"I'll wait for my husband," I said. There was no way I was going to be alone with William Kirby.

By the time Jack got off the phone with Doug we were more than ten minutes late, but I could see that whatever Doug had told Jack was important. Jack was almost bursting with it.

"This is going to be interesting," Jack said.

We followed Carissa up the stairs and I saw

William Kirby sitting at a corner table with a window view. His back was to the wall, which was where Jack normally would've sat.

Kirby got to his feet as we approached. "Thank you, Carissa."

Carissa brightened, seemingly grateful and impressed he remembered her name. "You're welcome, Mr. Kirby." She put menus in front of me and Jack and then made a hasty exit.

The way Kirby watched her walk away made my skin crawl.

"I thought a man of your upbringing would be more punctual," Kirby said in a scolding tone.

"Unfortunately," Jack said. "My timeline is sometimes determined by the victim. It's what the taxpayers pay me for."

"We all know you don't need the salary," Kirby said. His smile was one of comradery and mischief, letting Jack know he was aware of how things really worked and that it was okay to take short cuts from time to time.

But Jack didn't waver and he didn't share in the smile. "But the integrity and expectation is there just the same. A man died. We owe him everything we can give him."

"Hmm," Kirby said. "Related to the case with David?"

"We can't say at this point," Jack said.

"Of course you can," Kirby said, slapping his hands on the table impatiently. "I know all about your background." His icy gaze landed on me. "Yours too. What do you know about David's murder? If you're too incompetent to discover his killer then maybe it's time for someone else to take over."

"Mr. Kirby," Jack said, his voice smooth and easy. "I'm not sure what you thought this meeting would be. You agreed to come speak with us about your friends who were with you the night Sowers was killed. And if you really know anything about me, like you say you do, then you know you're wasting your time and your breath with blustery threats. You do not impress me. And neither does your job at the state department. And unless you are just ignorantly unaware of the law, then you know threatening to take this case elsewhere is never going to happen."

A dull flush of red crawled up Kirby's neck until I thought his head might pop off, but then he leaned his head back and laughed. The politician in him oozed from his pores, and he knew expertly how to regroup when something didn't go his way.

"I like you, son," Kirby said.

I felt Jack stiffen beside me, and I knew things were about to get interesting. The waitress chose that moment to bring our food.

"I ordered for all of us since you were late," Kirby said, flexing his importance again.

"I'll just have coffee," I told the waitress. "Black." There was no way I could stomach any food sitting across the table from that scumbag.

"Make that two," Jack said, holding up two fingers. "Who at the table Friday night has been with Sowers the longest?"

Kirby frowned, not liking that we'd rejected his order, but his face smoothed out as he thought about his answer.

"I guess that would be me," he said, laughing. "We've been friends for a long time now. I can't even remember how we met. But if you mean who's worked with him the longest that would probably be his admin, Colby. I think he's worked for David the last five years or so. David tended to have a high turnover in staff."

"Because of his drug use?" Jack asked.

Kirby smiled again and cut into his steak and eggs. "I don't know about any of that. But David was a demanding man. It's why he was so successful. He would've had a heck of a career in politics if he wanted it. He and his first wife could've been in the White House."

"If he hadn't killed that family while driving under the influence," Jack said.

"He was cleared of all charges," Kirby said.

"Because money buys things in this country that most people don't get. The same laws don't always apply. But what it shows is a pattern. He was an addict then without a care for anyone but himself and he's always been an addict, only his habit got more expensive. Who at the table knew about his penchant for young girls? You were his oldest friend, so besides you."

Jack slid it in so quickly it took Kirby a second to realize what he'd said. The red crept up from his neck again and I expected him to start foaming at the mouth.

"You see," Jack went on. "I have to keep going back to motive for his murder. It could've been the drugs. But Sowers wasn't a dealer, and no dealer in their right mind would cut off that kind of cash cow. So that leaves the trafficking. There's a lot of money involved there. But Sowers was getting sloppy. It's hard not to with his brains scrambled from cocaine. But now we have two dead veterans on our hands."

"Sounds like they were all involved with drugs to me," Kirby said, leaning back in his seat.

I could see him taking deep breaths, trying to get his temper under control. "Maybe David gave them a bad cut, or maybe they were his dealer and he didn't pay. Sounds like they took things into their own hands and used the skills they learned on the taxpayers' dime. It's a shame. It'll be a blemish on our military."

"It's going to be a blemish for a lot of people," Jack said. "I heard your name on the news this morning as being associated with Sowers. Even being in the same country as he was on several occasions while he was buying and selling girls. But I appreciate your version of the story. It's interesting, but I'm going to tell you what I think. I think maybe those soldiers had their own warped sense of justice. You see, I got a report back right before we walked in here that shows you and the soldier we found dead this morning were both at the US Embassy in Ukraine at the same time. He was working as a private contractor, but he's got a whole lot of special skills thanks to his time in the marines."

"Coincidence," Kirby said, waving his hand dismissively. "And I would love to see how you received your information. Military records are sealed."

Jack just smiled, but there was no humor in his eyes. "You want to hear another amazing coincidence? It turns out someone else who was at the Purple Pig Friday night was assigned to that same embassy with his Force RECON team. Apparently there was a skirmish of sorts that our media never picked up. Something about the daughter of a Russian diplomat accidentally being kidnapped and transported to our embassy. A terribly embarrassing mistake since you're quite well known for your frequent female visitors while traveling overseas on diplomatic missions. But negotiations were made and the United States lost a foothold in some very important foreign oil deals. How am I doing so far?"

Kirby used his napkin to wipe his mouth and then folded the napkin deliberately and placed it on his plate.

"I'll keep going," Jack said, settling in and enjoying himself. "There are more coincidences."

"I think I've heard enough," Kirby said.

"I'm not done," Jack said firmly. "You see, you and David Sowers coincidentally happened to be in the same country at the same time twenty-one times in the last five years alone. But guess who was signed in as a guest at the US Embassy the same night as you and Steven Machilenski?"

"Who the hell is Steven Machilenski?" Kirby yelled.

"He's the private contractor we just found

dead," Jack said harshly. "But David Sowers was there too. Are you going to tell me it's just a coincidence?" Jack didn't give him a chance to answer. "See, here's my theory. I've struggled with motive on this case from the beginning. But the more dead soldiers we find, the more things are starting to fall into place. You see, these soldiers knew the kind of man you were. They watched what you were doing and were sickened by it. They risked their lives every day and fought for their country and then someone like you comes along and makes a mockery of everything they fought for."

"Give me a break," Kirby said. "This country was built on capitalism."

"And freedom," Jack said. "You seemed to forget that as you're forcing girls away from their families and selling them to the highest bidder."

"Oh, you're one of those," Kirby said, shaking his head sadly. "Are you really so naïve after the career you've led? Stay in your lane, sheriff. You won't survive in the big leagues. You can't arrest me for murder, so our time here is done. And so what if Sowers and I had a side business? Do you know who some of our clients are? No one is going to stop me. I provide a service to a lot of very wealthy people."

Kirby got to his feet and looked down at us. "You don't mind picking up breakfast, do you?"

"I know you think that we can't touch you on criminal charges," Jack said. "And you're right. But rumor kills careers all the time. And there are a whole lot of rumors going around about you, and there will be even more on the evening news. How long do you think the president will allow your name to be associated with his, even on the periphery? Thanks for meeting with us today. You could've just stayed home and denied any involvement with anything regarding Sowers. But your ego and narcissism wouldn't let you. Whatever punishment you receive on this earth for the things you've done will never be enough. But fortunately you'll be spending an eternity in hell."

Kirby spun on his heel and strode away.

"He seems upset," I said, making Jack snort with laughter. "That must have been some phone call from Doug."

"You could say that," Jack said, digging for his wallet. "Guess who the other Force RECON guy was at the embassy."

"Well, we're running out of players," I said. "My choices are limited."

I was looking out the window, and my eye was drawn to Kirby as he came out the front door and bounded down the steps toward the parking lot. I had an uneasy feeling in my stomach, and was about to stand to my feet when Kirby's head jerked grotesquely and he crumpled to the ground, followed closely by the sound of a rifle firing.

CHAPTER SEVENTEEN

"THERE!" JACK SAID, POINTING TO THE CLOCK tower at the college. "That's where the shot will have come from."

Jack pulled out his phone and called dispatch, as we ran down toward the chaos.

"I need an APB on a J.D. Street. Shots fired from the clock tower at KGU. All available units begin cordoning off the area. Don't let him through the cracks. He's armed and dangerous. I need EMTs and a couple of units at The Big Over Easy in King George Proper. Single victim. GSW. I'm on-site with Dr. Graves."

We rushed through the screaming people on the main floor of the restaurant, most of them having taken cover at the first sound of a shot.

"Everyone stay down and keep quiet," Jack called out.

He put his hand on my arm, keeping me inside the restaurant. "Wait until we get clearance."

I nodded, noticing the few people who'd been in the parking lot were hunkered down by cars.

Jack's phone rang, and the sound seemed loud in the hushed panic of those around us.

"Lawson," he said.

I could hear dispatch on the other end of the line. Barbara Blanton had been manning the post for decades and she had a voice like a freight train.

"First on scene said the clock tower was clear," she said. "He must have been in and out of there in a jiffy because the closest unit was only two minutes away. They've got the streets blocked and will decrease the footprint as the search."

"I want a team at his house in case he goes back there," Jack said.

"You got it, boss," she said and hung up.

Two police units were turning into the parking lot along with an ambulance, and Jack and I pushed open the door and hurried over to where William Kirby lay.

"Back to the hollow point," Jack said. "Is your bag in the car?"

"Yeah," I said, already kneeling down to see what kind of damage the exit wound had done. I stood up and went back up the stairs, noticing the fragments buried in the outer wall of the restaurant. Jack came back a couple of minutes later with my bag.

"Thanks," I said, and hoisted the strap across my body.

"I hate to be impressed," Jack said. "But that was a really good shot. To hit a moving target from that distance...there aren't a lot of people in the world who could do that."

"I'm guessing J.D. was a sniper for the marines?" I asked, putting on a pair of gloves and kneeling down next to Kirby.

"He was part of an elite special ops unit," Jack said. "Just like Bobby Pickering."

"They were in at the same time?"

"No, but they were part of the same unit," Jack said. "Once a brother, always a brother. It doesn't matter that they didn't serve together. That special ops unit isn't big. They probably have private groups where they can help each other find jobs or places to live once they leave the service. Once Pickering was here it probably wasn't hard for J.D. to recruit him for providing a distraction the night Sowers was killed. And he and Steven Machilenski knew each other from their time in Ukraine. But J.D. was the brains behind this operation. He convinces the others that it's a noble pursuit. That it's up to them to protect and serve, even though they're no longer deployed. No one else is going to stop Kirby and Sowers, so why not them?"

"But then they killed Bobby," I said.

"J.D. would've convinced Steven that it was his turn to make the shot," Jack said. "They were both snipers, but J.D. was the better of the two. If they'd been competitive—and believe me, snipers are when it comes to kills—then it wouldn't have taken much for J.D. to goad Steven into taking out Pickering. J.D. made the first kill —a justified one in his eyes—so it was Steven's turn to kill Bobby. Also justified because it was common knowledge that Bobby suffered from PTSD. They knew he wouldn't be able to hold it together and keep the secret of who killed Sowers. So he had to go too. Sometimes you have to sacrifice the one to save the many."

I heard footsteps coming up the steps behind me, and I turned to see Cole and Martinez approaching. The affable look that was always on Martinez's face was gone and Cole looked down-right pissed.

"No sign of him yet," Cole said. "The responding officers on campus are checking every car and pedestrian. Most of the businesses are closed since it's Sunday, so we caught a break there. Not a lot of places to hide."

"How'd you figure out it was J.D.?" Martinez asked. "We heard the APB go out."

"Doug finally finessed his way through the military records of the veterans working for Denaro," Jack said.

He explained the connection between them and how they'd connected to Sowers and Kirby while in Ukraine.

"So Pickering does the drive-by to cause a diversion," Martinez said. "And J.D. is in the courthouse ready to take the shot. He's got an easy alibi with the car park thing and then comes back to the restaurant with Darnell. Where was Steven that night? Surely he wasn't really with his girlfriend."

"Getaway driver," Jack said. "The black SUV Pickering drove was left at the scene and his truck was found in the parking garage. He needed someone to pick him up so he could dump the car and get out of the Towne Square."

"So then Pickering decides to skip town," Martinez continued. "So he calls Darnell for help because he was never involved. But Steven is there to take him out before Pickering ruins it for them all. Only problem is a witness got a glimpse of him and the vehicle he was driving. So he goes home and puts a pistol to his temple."

"Or maybe J.D. helped him along," I said. "J.D. seems to like to tie up loose ends."

"And J.D. is the last man standing," Martinez said. "What could he hope to gain at this point? We have his identity and he's being hunted."

"We'll ask him when we find him," Jack said.

I moved aside so the EMTs could get in and we bagged Kirby and put him on the gurney for the trip to the lab. Lily and Sheldon would still be with Steven, so I knew there'd be no point in calling them in for this one. We could still only handle so many bodies at a time considering the size of our operation.

"Lily and Sheldon are at the funeral home," I told them. "They'll sign off on the paperwork."

They nodded and left us next to the blood-spattered steps.

The news about J.D. Street flooded the airwaves and media. There was a statewide manhunt for him, and there was nothing we could do but wait until he was spotted.

But there was a palpable fear in the air as we drove the streets back to Bloody Mary. People weren't lingering outside, and when they did have to go out they hurried to their destination as if there was a prize at the end. And the prize was living.

Even knowing that the targets had been only those who'd been part of what had happened in Ukraine didn't stop me from searching every rooftop as we passed. There was nothing to say J.D. might move to his next act of vigilantism now that he'd completed his first mission.

I could do more good at the funeral home than I could anywhere else, so that's where Jack was taking me. I had three autopsies and an embalming waiting for me. It was going to be a long night.

We'd just crossed into the Bloody Mary city limits when Jack's phone rang.

"Sheriff Lawson," he said.

"Sheriff, this is Alex Denaro. You gave me your number in case I had any information."

"Sure," Jack said. "What's going on?"

"I've been watching the news about J.D. About all my guys. I just can't believe it. They were good men. I swear to you I'd never have suspected anything like this. I can spot a con a mile away."

"It's okay, Denaro," Jack said. "I believe they were good men at one time. They just got a little misguided in what they were fighting for."

"You know how they all worked for Miller Construction?" Denaro asked, but didn't let Jack get a word in. "I might not have told you, but I'm half owner along with my cousin, and we're building a new subdivision over on Reformation Street."

"Yeah, we just passed it about five minutes ago," Jack said.

"I just got a call from the alarm company that the alarm was triggered a few minutes ago, so I went to check the cameras. We had to start using the cameras a couple years back because some of our subs kept walking off with supplies."

Jack had already done a U-turn in the middle of the street and was heading back toward Reformation Street while Denaro got to the point of his story.

"Anyway, I checked the cameras and sure enough, J.D. broke the back door and went right on in. It's our spec house too. It's already finished."

"What's the address?" Jack asked.

"Seventeen thirty-one," Denaro said. "You can't miss it. It's the first house on the left as you turn into the subdivision."

"Thanks," Jack said and disconnected. And then he dialed dispatch to ask for backup.

"Umm," I said as we pulled into the subdivision. "Are we really about to go up against a man who's been shooting people from a distance rather successfully?"

"We're going to drive by and assess," Jack said. "And then we're going to wait for backup. He can't kill us all with that rifle before someone rushes him."

"Comforting," I said. "I've always enjoyed a good game of Russian roulette."

Jack turned onto Reformation and there was a large two-story house on the left with an American flag waving from the top of a tall pole. There was a Miller Construction sign in the newly landscaped lawn and a black truck in the driveway. Jack drove past and kept going to the end of the street, where he turned around so he could see the house from a distance.

"You think he killed himself like Steven?" I asked.

"It's a possibility," Jack said. "What are his options at this point? Prison or death."

A cacophony of sirens blasted from all directions as cop cars barreled down the main road and turned onto the street. Several peeled off and went around to the alley, blocking all the exits.

Jack pulled the Tahoe back into the fray and we got out, moving around to the back.

Jack grabbed a bulletproof vest from his trunk and said, "Here, put this on."

It didn't seem like the time to bring up that J.D. seemed to excel at head shots, but I did as I was told and put on the vest. Martinez and Cole were on scene and everyone was getting prepped in case there was heavy fire. This was the part of the job I hated. Knowing that Jack time and time again would go into situations like this one. And one day he might not come out again.

"J.D. Street," Jack said, through the megaphone. "We've got the house surrounded. Come out with your hands up."

We waited for any signs of life inside the house, but there was no flutter of curtains or crack of a door. Jack motioned for Martinez and Cole to go around to the back, and they each peeled off in separate directions around the house.

"Captain Street," Jack repeated. "Come out with your hands up, soldier."

Cops were positioned behind their cars, using them as shields with their weapons drawn. Jack signaled for his cops to start moving two by two to the front and sides of the house. Jack had spent too many years in SWAT for him to let any man go in alone.

"Wait here," he said, giving me the megaphone and taking out his weapon. "I mean it. Stay down behind the Tahoe. I'll call you if we find a body."

And just that fast he was gone with the others, and they were moving through the front, side and back. Waiting wasn't my strong suit. I could hear yells as they cleared the areas, but then there was silence. A minute turned to two. And two minutes to five. Sweat trickled down my back and my hand cramped from how tight I was holding the megaphone.

I looked around, noticing Jack hadn't left me alone. There were others who'd been forced to endure the torture of waiting. Wachowski was a few feet away from me. I hadn't even had a chance to visit Plank since he'd been shot the day before. I couldn't imagine what she'd been going through since she'd gotten the news of Plank. Loving a cop was hard. Not everyone could do it.

"Why is it so quiet?" I whispered as I crept closer to her.

She was a small woman with flaming red hair that never stayed within the elastic band she habitually kept tied around it.

"I don't know," she said. "But I don't like it.

And I don't like that I got stuck out here with all the rookies."

I looked around at the other fresh-faced cops and grimaced. "You've got a lot going on with Plank. It's probably best you both don't get shot. One of you needs to be mobile in case he ever figures out what it means to have game."

"Oh, he's got game," Wachowski said. "You'd be surprised what lies dormant behind that choirboy face."

"I'm disturbed and fascinated," I said.

"You should try sleeping with him."

"Hard pass," I told her, and she snorted out a laugh. I felt some of the tension drain away.

A couple more minutes of silence passed and Wachowski and I looked at each other worriedly. All the cops who'd been left on the outside looked around. What were we missing? What was happening?"

Even as I had the thought, the front door opened and stoic-faced cops marched out. Then there was Martinez, followed by Cole who was holding a rifle in his hands. But there was no Jack. And there was no J.D.

I left the megaphone on the ground and got to my feet as Cole approached.

"Where's Jack?" I asked, trying not to let the panic creep out in my voice. "What's going on?"

"Jack's still in there with J.D.," Cole said. But there was something in the tone of his voice that had me pressing further.

"Why didn't he come out?" I asked. "What aren't you telling me?"

"When we breached the house J.D. was waiting for us inside," he said.

"I didn't hear any gunfire," I said, wiping my sweaty palms on my slacks.

"No," Cole said, glancing toward Martinez for backup. "He's strapped up with explosives. He wanted all of us to come in and get him so he could detonate."

I felt the air go out of my lungs and tiny black spots danced before my eyes. "Why is Jack still in there?" I could barely get the words out.

"Because Jack is a trained negotiator," Martinez said. "He's a psychologist. He got J.D. to let the rest of us go before things could escalate too quickly."

"You left him there!" I asked, moving in close to Cole. "How could you leave him? He would have never left you. Never."

The look on Cole's face was pained, but he said, "He ordered us to leave, Jaye. And if we didn't we could have undone everything he'd been working toward. All we can do is wait for this to play out."

I pressed my hands flat down on the hood of the car as hard as I could, trying to anchor myself to whatever this weird reality was I was living. Martinez and Cole stood on either side of me, and I didn't know how many minutes passed. I just knew each extra second put me further away from Jack. And each extra minute made it more of a possibility that I'd never see him again.

I focused on every breath coming in and out of my lungs, and I prayed like I never had before, willing Jack to walk through that front door.

I wasn't sure what made my knees buckle first —the giant fireball that swept through the house or the deafening concussion of the explosion as the house splintered into a million difference pieces.

Something sharp cut my cheek, but I barely felt the sting as I went to my hands and knees. All the air had left my body, and the only thing in its place was a pain so unimaginable any kind of torture would've been preferable.

I curled into the smallest ball I could muster and willed the rest of the world to go away. I felt arms trying to lift me to my feet and the sound of orders being shouted to move back, but I would have been okay with the fire swallowing me whole.

Arms tightened around me and lifted me into

the air, and I looked up into Cole's devastated face. Blood dripped from the corner of his eye and his face was dirty.

There was nothing but smoke and flame in front of us, and the fire trucks had arrived. The cold wind was making the smoke dance and spread, and it was then I saw a lone figure walking toward me.

"I'm dead," I said.

"What?" Cole asked.

"I think we're all dead," I told him and pointed.

Cole turned and put me carefully to my feet as Jack's face came into view. It was black with smoke and soot, and there was blood dripping freely down his neck.

"She thinks we're all dead," Cole told him. And then Cole grabbed Jack in a bear hug and said, "Boy, are you a sight for sore eyes."

"I'm not dead," Jack told me, his gaze never leaving mine.

"I don't understand," I said, not quite brave enough to reach out and touch him yet. "How?"

"I'd convinced J.D. to do the honorable thing and turn himself in," Jack said. "He took off the explosives vest and laid it on the chair. And then I took him out the back door because I could see Riley and Chen through the window and it seemed a faster way to get him out. But I guess the vest had a hair trigger and it blew when we were about halfway to the squad car. We both flew a little bit from the blast."

The first sob caught me by surprise. And then it seemed it was all I could do. I crumpled where I stood, but Jack caught me and went to the ground with me.

"I can't ever go through that again, Jack Lawson," I said. "Don't ever put yourself at risk like that again. I mean it."

"I know you do," he said, sighing into my hair. "You used my full name."

"I'm not kidding," I said, the pitch of my voice leaning toward hysterical. "I thought I was tough. That I would always be okay on my own. But you've ruined that. Now I can't stand the thought of living without you."

"Oh, baby," he said, resting his head on my shoulder. "All I could think while I was in there was that I had a tremendous responsibility. To you first. But also to all the men and women who were trusting me with their lives. All I could think was that I had to get them out, no matter the cost."

"Always the bloody hero," I said, sobbing even harder.

"That didn't sound like a compliment."

"I know you're a hero," I said. "That's just one of the many things about you I fell in love with. I just want to be selfish for once. I want you to be selfish for once and let someone else be the hero. But I know this conversation is like spitting into the wind. Asking you to stop being a hero or doing the right or responsible thing would be like asking you to stop breathing."

I wiped my hands across my face and they came away with ash and blood.

"I'm sorry," he said. "I wish this calling on my life didn't make you hurt so bad."

"Just ignore me," I said. "I'm overly emotional and feeling a little crazy at the moment. I'm still trying to come to grips that I didn't just watch you die in a fiery explosion. It's just a small pity party. I'll be over it in a second or ten."

"How about you just let me sit here and hold you for a little while?" he asked. "And you can take all the time you need to make sure that I'm alive."

EPILOGUE

I WAS STILL SITTING AT THE BAR IN THE KITCHEN with the postcard in my hand when Jack came in. There was a white bandage on his jaw, and he was going to have some pretty colorful bruises. But he was alive and we were together. That's what mattered.

"What's that?" he asked, taking the barstool next to mine.

"I don't know," I said. "It was in the mail. Who do we know who would send a postcard from Hong Kong?"

Jack sighed and took the postcard and turned it over. It was blank except for six tally marks in the top left corner and our name and address in the center.

"Carver," Jack said. "Carver got his wife and kids to Hong Kong."

"Is that good?" I asked, confused. "How do you know?"

"The tally marks," Jack said. "There are six of them. They're all together. And yes, Hong Kong is good for a couple of reasons. The CIA has a large operation there. And they also don't have an extradition treaty with the United States. It's probably the safest place he and Michelle and the kids could be right now until they get the whole mess figured out."

"Do you think they'll figure it out?"

"I think it's going to be very messy for some very important people," Jack said. "I've known Carver a long time. I know him well enough to be sure that he'll always do the right thing. And I know him well enough to guarantee that he doesn't care about diplomacy. He'll start leaking information so egregious that no one will be able to hide behind the normal political rhetoric. We just need to be ready with the popcorn."

"I wish I knew what was going on," I said. "He told me it all started with Floyd Parker."

"Carver told you that?" Jack asked, arching a brow.

"Yeah, that day he was here. He said he discovered some things he wasn't supposed to while he was digging into Floyd during the election."

Jack shrugged. "Carver's a big boy. He'll get it all sorted out. And he'll stay in touch one way or another so we know he's okay. Besides, we've got our own lives to sort out."

"I'm ready to have a baby," I blurted out.

Jack looked like someone had punched him between the eyes. "Right now?"

"I mean I'm ready to start trying," I said. "It's time. If we keep waiting and working cases we'll never have a family. What we do will never get easier, and the world is not going to slow down and get less crazy. But we can control the level of crazy we allow into our lives."

"Okay," Jack said, his gaze direct and serious.

"That's it?" I asked. "Just okay?"

"I've always wanted children with you," he said. "I was just waiting on you to realize you wanted children with me."

"I never thought I'd be a good mom," I said, shrugging. "I didn't exactly have the best example. And I'll probably screw up a lot. But I trust you, and I know you won't let me screw it up too bad. This last case scared me. We both could have died. I keep wondering how much longer we'll be able to cheat death."

It wasn't as easy to admit that as I thought it

would be. "I've come close to death before, but at that point in my life I didn't have quite so much to lose. We've got to be more careful. You're the sheriff. You don't have to be on every crime scene. That's why you have detectives. And my job is to show up on the scene after the danger is gone. It's been fun solving crimes together. But you're getting burned out and I'm starting to wonder what our purpose is. Maybe it's time to take a break and just do the jobs we're supposed to do and come home at the end of the day."

Jack leaned his arms on the bar and dropped his head. I didn't like not seeing his face or his reaction to what I had said. It had probably felt like a bombshell had been dropped. Then he pushed up and grabbed my hand.

"Let's make a deal," Jack said. "We'll start trying for a baby." He winked at me and said, "I've got the next couple of hours free."

"Romantic," I said.

"You want romance or you want to make a baby?" he asked.

I laughed and shook my head, tucking my hair behind my ear. He could always make me laugh.

"I want both," I said.

"Fortunately you're married to a man who can do both." He rubbed his thumb over the simple band on my finger and said, "Here's the deal. When you get pregnant, you become just a coroner and funeral home director and I become just the sheriff, and we clock out at regular times and have all of our weekends free. We give this kid as normal of a life as possible, and try not to make her neurotic about stranger danger and social awareness."

"Her?" I asked.

"I want a girl first," he said.

"First?"

He just smiled.

"You said when I get pregnant," I said.

"What do you mean?" he asked.

"You said we'd be normal and have normal schedules when I get pregnant."

"We are normal. I didn't say we're not normal."

"You know what I mean," I said. "And we are kind of abnormal. But in a good way." I shook my head. "Stop distracting me. My point is you said we'd go to that schedule after I get pregnant. What are we doing in the meantime?"

"I've got some ideas on that," Jack said. "Starting with both of us taking a few vacation days and going somewhere warm. This has been the longest February in the history of time. And then when we come back I suggest you start looking for some more help at the funeral home. Someone to work weekends and nights. You never know how long it'll take us to make a baby, but we'll give it our best shot. And if a case comes along that seems interesting and not too dangerous..."

I arched a brow as he left the sentence hanging. "I can deal with that," I said. "Interesting and not too dangerous. Something like that rarely comes along."

"Rarely," he agreed. "But if it does..."

"We're on the case," I said. "We're a good team."

He stood and pulled me up. "The best." And then he scooped me up into his arms.

"What are you doing?" I asked, giggling.

"You said you wanted romance."

It was hard to disagree with that.

ABOUT THE AUTHOR

Liliana Hart is a *New York Times*, *USA Today*, and Publisher's Weekly bestselling author of more than eighty titles. After starting her first novel her freshman year of college, she immediately became addicted to writing and knew she'd found what she was meant to do with her life. She has no idea why she majored in music.

Since publishing in June 2011, Liliana has sold more than ten-million books. All three of her series have made multiple appearances on the *New York Times* list.

Liliana can almost always be found at her computer writing, hauling five kids to various activities, or spending time with her husband. She calls Texas home.

If you enjoyed reading this, I would appreciate it if you would help others enjoy this book, too.

Recommend it. Please help other readers find this book by recommending it to friends, readers' groups and discussion boards.

Review it. Please tell other readers why you liked this book by reviewing.

Connect with me online:
www.lilianahart.com

facebook.com/LilianaHart

instagram.com/LilianaHart

bookbub.com/authors/liliana-hart

ALSO BY LILIANA HART

JJ Graves Mystery Series

Dirty Little Secrets

A Dirty Shame

Dirty Rotten Scoundrel

Down and Dirty

Dirty Deeds

Dirty Laundry

Dirty Money

A Dirty Job

Dirty Devil

Playing Dirty

Dirty Martini

Dirty Dozen

Dirty Minds

Addison Holmes Mystery Series

Whiskey Rebellion

Whiskey Sour

Whiskey For Breakfast

Whiskey, You're The Devil

Whiskey on the Rocks

Whiskey Tango Foxtrot

Whiskey and Gunpowder

Whiskey Lullaby

The Scarlet Chronicles

Bouncing Betty

Hand Grenade Helen

Front Line Francis

The Harley and Davidson Mystery Series

The Farmer's Slaughter

A Tisket a Casket

I Saw Mommy Killing Santa Claus

Get Your Murder Running

Deceased and Desist

Malice in Wonderland

Tequila Mockingbird

Gone With the Sin

Grime and Punishment

Blazing Rattles

A Salt and Battery

Curl Up and Dye

First Comes Death Then Comes Marriage

Made in the USA
Columbia, SC
30 May 2023